STORIES FROM ANDERSEN

CHILDREN'S
CLASSICS

STORIES FROM
ANDERSEN

Hans Christian Andersen

Bloomsbury Books
London

This edition published 1993 by Bloomsbury Books, an imprint
of The Godfrey Cave Group, 42 Bloomsbury Street, London,
WC1B 3QJ.

ISBN 1 85471 240 3

Printed and bound by Imprimerie Hérissey, France.
N° d'impression : 24968

Contents

The Six Swans

A King one day went hunting in the forest, and he chased
a deer so far and fast that nobody could keep up with
him. When evening came, he halted and looked around
to see where he was, and knew that he was lost. He
looked in vain for a way out of the woods. Then he saw
an old woman sitting in a hollow tree: she was a witch.

"My good woman," he said to her, "can you show me a
way out of the woods?"

"I can easily do that, O King," she answered, "but on
one condition. If you don't agree to it you'll never get
out, but will die of hunger here."

"And what is the condition?" asked the King.

"I have a daughter," said the old woman; "she is very
beautiful and worthy to be your wife. If you will make
her your Queen I will show you the way out of the wood."

The King, in his distress, agreed, and the old woman
took him to her hut, where her daughter, who was sitting
by the fire, welcomed the King as if she had expected
him. Beautiful indeed she was, and yet he could not look
at her without horror. When he had lifted her on to his
horse, the old woman showed him the path, and by and
by he reached the royal castle, where the wedding took
place.

Now the King had been married before, and his first
wife had left him seven children, six boys and a girl,
whom he loved more than anything else in the world. As

he was afraid that their stepmother might treat them badly and do them harm, he took them to a lonely castle in the middle of a forest. It was in such a secret place that he would not himself have been able to find it, had not a wise woman given him a ball of magic yarn; when he threw it down before him, it unwound itself and led the way.

Well, the King visited his dear children so often that his wife noticed it, and grew inquisitive to know what he was doing in the woods. So she paid his servants a lot of money to tell her the secret, and they told her also about the magic yarn. After that she had no rest till she knew where the King hid the ball. Then she made little white shirts of silk, and as she had learned witchcraft from her mother, she sewed a spell into each.

One day, when the King had gone hunting, she took the shirts and went into the wood, with the ball of yarn to show her the way. When the boys heard somebody coming, they thought it was their dear father, and ran joyfully to meet him. Then she threw one of the little shirts over each, and as soon as it touched him he turned into a swan which flew away over the forest.

She went home pleased to think she had got rid of her stepchildren, but the girl had not run out with her brothers, and the Queen knew nothing about her.

Next day, when the King went to visit his children, he found only the little girl.

"Where are your brothers?" he asked.

"Oh, father dear," she answered, "they have gone away and left me alone," and she told him how from her little window she had seen her brothers turn into swans and fly off over the trees, and showed him the feathers which they had let fall in the courtyard, and which she had picked up.

The King was full of sorrow, but he never guessed that this was the Queen's wicked work, and as he feared lest the little girl also should be stolen away, he made up his mind to take her with him: but she was afraid of her stepmother, and begged her father to leave her for one more night in the castle in the woods.

For the poor little girl thought to herself: "This is no place for me to stay. I shall go off to seek my brothers," and when night came she fled away into the forest. She kept on walking all night and the next day till she was too tired to go any farther, and when she came to a hut, she went in and found a room with six little beds in it. She didn't like to lie down on any of them, but instead crept underneath one, to spend the night on the hard floor. Just before sunset she heard a rushing of wings, and then six swans flew in at the window. They settled down on the floor and blew upon one another, and blew all the feathers off, and their swan-skins came off like shirts.

The little girl watched, and recognized her brothers, and joyfully crept out from under the bed. When her brothers saw her, they were as happy as she, but their happiness did not last long.

"You mustn't stay here," they told her. "This is a robbers' hut, and when they come back they will kill you."

"Can't you protect me?" asked their little sister.

"No," they answered, "for we can take off our swan-shirts and appear as ourselves for only a quarter of an hour every evening, then we are turned back into swans."

Their little sister cried and asked, "Can't you anyhow be set free?"

"Ah, no," they replied, "the conditions are too difficult—for six years you would have neither to speak nor smile, and during that time make us six shirts out of daisies. If you spoke one single word, all the work would go for nothing."

No sooner had her brothers told her this than the quarter of an hour was over, and off they flew through the window, swans again.

Then the little girl made a great resolve: she would set her brothers free though it should cost her her life! She left the hut, went out into the forest, and spent the night sitting in a tree. In the morning she gathered daisies and began to sew them together. She must not speak to anybody: she did not feel like smiling: she just sat there in the tree and worked.

It happened that the King of that country was hunting in the woods, and after the little girl had been sitting there for a long time, his huntsmen came to the tree where she sat. One shouted to her, "Who are you?" but she gave no answer. "Come down," they called, "we won't hurt you." She only shook her head. As they kept on troubling her with questions, she took off her golden necklace and threw it down to them, hoping they would be content to have that and go away. Then, as they kept on questioning, she threw down her jewelled girdle, and one by one all her fine things till she had nothing left but her plain smock.

Even then the huntsmen wouldn't go away: they climbed the tree, carried her down, and took her to the King.

The King asked her, "Who are you? What were you doing up in the tree?" but she gave no reply.

He questioned her in all the languages he knew, but she kept as dumb as a fish.

Now she was very pretty, and the King was falling in love with her, so he wrapped her in his cloak, placed her before him on his horse, and took her home to his castle. There she was dressed in splendid garments, so that her beauty shone like a sunny day, but not one word would she speak.

She sat at the King's side at table, and her fine manners and noble air so pleased him that he said, "This is she I mean to marry, and no other girl in the world," and the wedding took place a few days later.

But the King's mother was wicked: she did not like the marriage and talked against the young Queen.

"Who knows anything about the chit?" she said. "She can't speak: she's not worthy of the King."

When a year later the first royal baby was born, the wicked old woman took it away and told the King that the Queen had killed it. This the King would not believe, and he would not allow any harm to be done to his wife. Meanwhile she sat silent and went on sewing calmly.

The following year another baby was born, a beautiful boy. The wicked mother-in-law played the same trick, but still the King couldn't bring himself to believe her story.

"My Queen is too good and gentle," he said, "to do such a thing, and if she were not dumb she would prove her innocence."

But when, for the third time, the old woman took away a new-born baby and accused the Queen, who spoke not a word to defend herself, the King could do nothing but send her before the judges, who condemned her to be burned.

Now the day on which she was to die was the very last day of the six years in which she was not to speak or to smile, and so she had saved her dear brothers from the spell. The six shirts were finished all but the left sleeve of the last.

When the time came for her to be driven to the place where she must die, she put the six shirts over her arm, and then, when the fire was about to be lit, she looked all around, and there came six swans speeding through the air!

So she knew that the hour of their freedom had come, and her heart swelled with joy.

The swans dived down to her and drew so close that she was able to throw the shirts over them: and all, as the shirts touched them, threw off the likeness of swans and stood up before her, gay and handsome. (Only the youngest lacked a left arm: a swan's wing rose from his shoulder instead.)

They kissed and petted their sister, who went to the King and told him everything. "Dearest husband, at last I may speak and make you understand that I am not guilty, but falsely accused," and she told the King of the old woman's trick, and how it was she who had taken away the babies and hidden them. And to the King's great joy they were brought back. The wicked old woman was condemned to be burned to ashes, and the King and Queen and her six brothers lived many many years in peace and happiness.

The Red Shoes

There was once a little girl, very pretty and delicate, but so poor that in summer she always went barefoot, and in winter wore large wooden shoes that made her little ankles quite red and sore.

In the same village lived an old shoemaker's wife. One day she made out of some old pieces of red cloth a pair of little shoes. They were clumsy certainly, but they fitted the little girl fairly well, and she gave them to her. The little girl's name was Karen.

It was on the day of her mother's funeral that the red shoes were given to Karen. They were not at all proper for mourning, but she had no others, and in them she walked with bare legs behind the poor deal coffin.

Just then a large old carriage rolled by. In it sat a large old lady who saw the little girl and pitied her, and she said to the priest, "Give me the little girl, and I will take care of her."

Karen thought it was for the sake of the red shoes that the old lady had taken a fancy to her; but the old lady thought them frightful, and so they were burnt. And Karen was dressed very neatly, and was taught to read and to work; and people told her she was pretty. But the mirror said, "You are more than pretty; you are beautiful!"

One day the Queen with her little daughter passed through the town where Karen lived, and all the people, Karen amongst them, crowded in front of the palace, whilst the little princess stood, dressed in white, at a window, for every one to see her. She wore neither train nor gold crown; but on her feet were pretty red morocco shoes—much prettier indeed than those the shoemaker's wife had made for little Karen. Nothing in the world could be compared with these red shoes!

Karen was now old enough to be confirmed. She was to have a new frock and new shoes. The rich shoemaker in the town took the measure of her little foot. He took the measure in his own room where there was a large glass case full of neat shoes and shining boots. They looked very pretty, but the old lady, whose sight was not very good, did not notice them much. Amongst the shoes was a pair of red ones, just like those worn by the Princess. The shoemaker said they had been made for a Count's daughter but did not fit.

"They are of polished leather," said the old lady; "see how they shine!"

"Yes, they shine beautifully!" exclaimed Karen. And as the shoes fitted her, they were bought. But the old lady did not know that they were red, or she would never have suffered Karen to go to confirmation in them. But Karen did go. Everybody looked at her feet, and as she walked up the nave to the chancel it seemed to her that even the stone figures on the tombstones, and the portraits of the pastors and their wives with their stiff ruffs and long black robes, fixed their eyes on her red shoes. When she knelt before the altar she thought only of them; even when the clergyman laid his hand on her head, and when he spoke of her baptism, of her covenant with God, and of how she must remember that she was now a full grown Christian. The organ sent forth its deep, solemn tones, the children's sweet voices mingled with those of the choristers, but Karen still thought only of her red shoes.

That afternoon, when the old lady was told that Karen had worn red shoes at her confirmation, she was vexed, and told Karen that for the future when she went to church, she must wear black shoes, were they ever so old.

On the next Sunday Karen was to make her first communion. She looked first at the red shoes, then at the black, then at the red again, and—put them on.

It was beautiful sunshiny weather, so Karen and the old lady walked to church through the corn-fields, for the road was dusty.

At the church door stood an old soldier with a strange reddish-coloured beard. He was leaning on crutches, and he bowled almost to the earth, and asked the old lady if he might wipe the dust off her shoes. Karen put out her little foot also. "Oh, what pretty dancing-shoes!" said the old soldier; "mind you do not let them slip off when you dance;" and he passed his hands over them.

The old lady gave the soldier some money, and then went with Karen into church.

Again every one looked at Karen's red shoes; and all the carved figures bent their gaze upon them. And when Karen knelt before the altar, the red shoes still floated before her eyes. She thought of them and of them only, and she forgot to join in the hymn of praise—she forgot to repeat the Lord's Prayer.

At last all the people came out of church, and the old lady got into her carriage. Karen was lifting her foot to follow, when the old soldier standing in the porch cried, "Only look, what pretty dancing-shoes!" And then Karen found she could not help dancing a few steps. And after she had begun, her feet kept moving of themselves as though the shoes had a power over them. She danced round the churchyard and could not stop. The coachman was obliged to run after her, take hold of her and lift her into the carriage; but even then the feet kept on dancing, so that the good old lady got many a hard kick. At last the shoes were taken off, and the feet had rest.

Then the shoes were put away in a press, but Karen could not help going to look at them every now and then.

After a while the old lady lay ill in bed, and the doctor said she would never get better. She needed careful nursing, and who should have been her nurse and constant attendant but Karen? But there was to be a grand ball in the town, and Karen was invited. She thought of the dying old lady, she looked at the red shoes, and then she thought there could be no harm in putting them on. Then she went to the ball and began to dance. But when she wanted to move to the right, the shoes bore her to the left; and when she would dance up the room, the shoes danced down the room, danced down the stairs, through the streets, and through the gates of the town. She danced on in spite of herself, till she danced into the dark wood.

Something shone through the trees. She thought at first it must be the moon shining through the mist. Then she saw a face; it was the old soldier with the red beard. He sat there nodding at her, and repeating, "See what pretty dancing-shoes they are!"

She was frightened, and tried to pull off her red shoes, but they were stuck fast to her feet. She tore off her stockings but the shoes seemed to have grown on to her feet. She felt compelled to go on dancing over field and meadow, in rain and in sunshine, by night and by day. It was most terrible at night. She danced across the open churchyard. The dead do not dance, they have something better to do. She would fain have sat down on the poor man's grave, where the bitter ferns grew, but for her there was neither rest nor quiet. She danced past the open church door, and there she saw an angel, clad in long white robes, and with wings that reached from his shoulders to the ground. His face was grave and stern, and in his hand he held a bright, glittering sword.

"Dance on," said he; "dance on, in thy red shoes, till thou art pale and cold, and thy skin shrinks and shrivels up like a skeleton's. Thou shalt dance still, from door to door, and wherever proud, vain children live thou shalt knock, so that they may hear thee and be afraid. Dance shalt thou, dance on—"

"Mercy!" cried Karen. But she heard not the angel's answer, for the shoes carried her through the gate, into the fields, along highways and byways; and still she had to dance on.

One morning she danced past a door she knew well. She heard psalm-singing within, and saw a coffin, strewn with flowers, borne out. Then Karen knew that the good old lady was dead, and she felt herself a thing forsaken by men, and condemned by the Angel of God.

Still, on she felt forced to dance, even into the dark night. The shoes bore her through thorns and briers, till her limbs were torn and bleeding. Then she danced across the heath to a little lonely house where she knew the headsman lived; and she tapped with her fingers against the panes, crying:

"Come out! come out! I cannot come in for I must dance."

And the headsman said, "Surely you do not know who I am! I cut off the heads of wicked men; and I notice that my axe is quivering."

"Do not cut off my head," said Karen, "for then I could not live to repent of my sin; but cut off my feet with the red shoes."

Then she confessed all her sins, and the headsman cut off her feet with the red shoes on them; and the shoes with those little feet in them danced away over the fields, and into the deep forests.

Then the headsman made her a pair of wooden feet, and cut down some branches to serve as crutches, and he taught her the psalm which the penitents sing. And she kissed the hand that held the axe, and limped away over the heath. "Now I have certainly suffered quite enough through the red shoes," thought Karen, "I still go to church and let people see me once more." And she went as fast as she could to the church porch; but as she drew near it, the red shoes danced before her, and she was frightened and turned her back.

All that week she was sorrowful and shed many bitter

tears. Then when Sunday came, she said to herself, "Now I have suffered and striven enough; I dare say I am quite as good as many of those who are holding their heads so high in church." So she took heart and went; but she did not get farther than the churchyard gate, for there again she saw the red shoes dancing before her, and in great terror she turned back, and repented more deeply than ever of her sinful pride.

Then she went to the pastor's house, and begged that some work might be given her, promising to work hard and do all she could even without wages. She only wanted a roof to shelter her, she said, and to dwell with good people. And the pastor's wife had pity on her, and took her into her service. And Karen was grateful and industrious.

Every evening she sat silently listening to the pastor while he read the Bible aloud. All the children loved her, but when she heard them talk about dress and finery, and about being as beautiful as a queen, she would sorrowfully shake her head.

Next Sunday all the pastor's household went to church; and they asked her to go too; but she sighed, and looked with tears in her eyes upon her crutches.

When they were all gone, she went into her own little room, which was just large enough to hold a bed and a chair, and there she sat with her psalm-book in her hand and, as she read in a humble and devout spirit, the wind wafted to her the sound of the organ from the church, and she lifted up her tearful face and prayed, "O God, help me!"

Then the sun shone brightly, and before her stood the white-robed Angel of God, the same whom she had seen on that night of horror at the church porch. But he no longer held in his hand a threatening sword; he carried instead a lovely green branch covered with roses. With this he touched the ceiling, which at once rose to a great height, and a bright gold star glittered on the spot the green branch had touched. He touched the walls too, and they opened wide, and Karen saw the organ, the old monuments, and the congregation all sitting in their richly carved seats and singing from their psalm-books.

For the church had come home to the poor girl in her narrow room, or rather the room had grown a church to her. She sat with the rest of the pastor's servants, and, when the psalm was ended, they looked up and nodded to her, saying, "You did well to come, Karen!"

"It was through mercy I came," said she.

And then the organ pealed forth again, and with it the children's voices in the choir rose clear and sweet. The sunbeams streamed through the windows and fell bright and warm on Karen's seat. Her heart was so full of sunshine, of peace and gladness, that it broke; and her soul flew upon a sunbeam to her Father in heaven, where not a look of reproach awaited her, not a word was breathed of the red shoes.

The Constant Tin Soldier

There were once five and twenty tin soldiers, all brothers, for all had been made out of one old tin spoon. They carried muskets in their arms, and held themselves very upright, and their uniforms were red and blue. The first words they heard in this world were, "Tin soldiers!" It was a little boy who uttered them, when the lid was taken off the box where they lay; and he clapped his hands with delight. They had been given to him because it was his birthday. Then he set them out on the table.

The soldiers were like each other to a hair; all but one, who had only one leg, because he had been made last, when there was not quite enough tin left. He stood as firmly, however, upon his one leg as the others did upon their two; and it is this one-legged tin soldier's fortunes that seem to us worthy of being told.

On the table where the tin soldiers stood there were other playthings, but the most charming of them all was a pretty pasteboard castle. Through its little windows one could look into the rooms. In front of the castle stood some tiny trees, clustering round a little mirror intended to represent a lake. Some waxen swans swam on the lake and were reflected in it.

All this was very pretty, but prettiest of all was a little lady standing in the open doorway of the castle. She, too, was cut out of pasteboard, but she had on a frock of the softest muslin, and a narrow sky-blue riband was flung across her shoulders like a scarf, and in the middle of this scarf was set a glittering tinsel rose. The little lady was a dancer, and she stretched out both her arms, and raised one of her legs so high in the air that the tin soldier could not see it, and thought she had, like himself, only one leg.

"That would be just the wife for me," thought he, "but then she is of too high a rank. She lives in a castle, and I have only a box; and even that is not my own, for all our five and twenty men live in it; so it is no place for her. Still, I must make her acquaintance." Then he laid himself down at full length behind a snuf-box that stood on the table so that he had a full view of the delicate little lady still standing on one leg without losing her balance.

When evening came, all the other tin soldiers were put into the box, and the people of the house went to bed. Then the playthings began to have their own games; to pay visits, to fight battles, and to give balls. The tin soldiers rattled in the box, for they wished to play too, but the lid would not open. The nut-crackers cut capers, and the slate-pencil danced about on the table. There was such a noise that the canary woke up and began to talk too; but he always talked in verse. The only two who did not move from their places were the tin soldier and the dancer. She remained standing on the very tip of her toes, with outstretched arms; and he stood just as firmly on his one leg, never for a moment taking his eyes off her.

Twelve o'clock struck, and with a crash the lid of the snuff-box sprang open—there was no snuff in it, it was

only a toy puzzle—and out jumped a little black conjurer. "Tin soldier!" said the conjurer, "please keep your
eyes to yourself!"

But the tin soldier pretended not to hear.

"Well, just wait till tomorrow!" said the conjurer.

When the children got up next morning the tin soldier
was placed on the window-ledge, and, whether the conjurer or the wind caused it, all at once the window flew
open, and out fell the tin soldier, head foremost, from the
third storey to the ground. It was a dreadful fall, for he
fell head first into the street, and at last rested with his
cap and bayonet stuck between two paving-stones, and
with his one leg in the air.

The servant-maid and the little boy came downstairs
directly to look for him; but though they very nearly trod
on him they could not see him. If the tin soldier had but
called out, "Here I am!" they might easily have found
him; but he thought it would not be becoming for him to
cry out, as he was in uniforrn.

Presently it began to rain; soon the drops were falling
thicker, and there was a perfect downpour. When it was
over, two little street arabs came by.

"Look," said one, "there is a tin soldier. Let him have a
sail for once in his life."

So they made a boat out of newspaper, and put the tin
soldier into it. Away he sailed down the gutter, both the
boys running along by the side of it and clapping their
hands. The paper boat rocked to and fro, and every now
and then was whirled round so quickly that the tin soldier
becarne quite giddy. Still he did not move a muscle but

looked straight before him, and held his musket tightly
clasped.

All at once the boat was carried into a long drain, where
the tin soldier found it as dark as in his own box.

"Where can I be going now?" thought he. "It is all that
conjurer's doing. Ah! if only the little maiden were sailing with me I would not mind its being twice as dark."

Just then a great water-rat that lived in the drain darted
out. "Have you a passport?" asked the rat. "Show me
your passport!" But the tin soldier was silent, and held
his musket tighter than ever. The boat sailed on, and the
rat followed. How he gnashed his teeth, and cried out to
the sticks and the straws: "Stop him, stop him, he has not
paid his toll; he has not even shown his passport." But
the stream grew stronger and stronger. The tin soldier
could already catch a glimpse of the daylight where the
tunnel ended, but at the same time he heard a roaring
noise that might have made the boldest tremble. Where
the tunnel ended, the water of the gutter fell into a great
canal. This was as dangerous for the tin soldier as a
waterfall would be for us.

The fall was now so close that he could no longer stand
upright. The boat darted forward; the poor tin soldier
held himself as stiffly as possible; so that no one could
accuse him of having even blinked. The boat span round
three or four times, and was filled with water to the brim;
it must sink now.

The tin soldier stood up to his neck in water; but deeper
and deeper sank the boat, and softer and softer grew the
paper till the water stood over the soldier's head. He

thought of the pretty little dancer whom he should never see again, and these words rang in his ears:—

> *Fare on, thou soldier brave!*
> *Life must end in the grave.*

The paper now split in two, and the tin soldier fell through the rent and was at once swallowed up by a large fish. Oh, how dark it was! darker even than in the tunnel and much narrower too! But the tin soldier was as constant as ever; and lay there at full length, still shouldering his arms.

The fish swam to and fro, and made the strangest movements, but at last he became quite still. After a while a flash of lightning seemed to dart through him and the daylight shone brightly, and some one cried out, "I declare, here is the tin soldier!" The fish had been caught, taken to the market, sold and brought into the kitchen, where the servant-girl was cutting him up with a large knife. She seized the tin soldier by the middle with two of her fingers, and took him into the parlour, where every one was eager to see the wonderful man who had travelled in the maw of a fish. But the tin soldier was not proud.

They set him on the table, and—what strange things do happen in the world!—the tin soldier was in the very room in which he had been before. He saw the same children, the same plaything on the table—among them the beautiful castle with the pretty little dancing maiden, who was still standing upon one leg, while she held the other high in the air; she too was constant. It quite touched the tin soldier; he could have found it in his heart to weep tin tears, but such weakness would have been unbecoming in a soldier. He looked at her and she looked at him, but neither spoke a word.

And now one of the boys took the soldier and threw him into the stove. He gave no reason for doing so; but no doubt it was the fault of the conjurer in the snuff-box.

The tin soldier now stood in a blaze of light. He felt extremely hot, but whether from the fire or from the flames of love he did not know. He had entirely lost his colour. Whether this was the result of his travels, or the effect of strong feeling, I know not. He looked at the little lady, and she looked at him, and he felt that he was melting; but, constant as ever, he still stood shouldering his arms. A door opened, and the draught caught the dancer; and, like a sylph, she flew straightway into the stove, to the tin soldier. Instantly she was in a blaze and was gone. The soldier was melted and dripped down among the ashes, and when the maid cleaned out the fireplace the next day she found his remains in the shape of a little tin heart. Of the dancer all that was left was the tinsel rose, and that was as black as coal.

Thumbykin

There was once a woman who wished very much for a little child, but did not know where to find one. So at last she went to a witch and said to her: "I do so much wish to have a little child; can you, who are so wise, tell me where I can find one?"

"I can readily do so," said the witch. "There is nothing easier. Here is a barley corn, but it is quite unlike those that grow in the farmers' fields and that the fowls eat. Put it into a flower-pot and wait and see what takes place."

"Oh, thank you so much," said the woman, giving the witch twelve shillings, which was the price she asked for her barley corn. Thereafter she went straight home and planted the barley corn, and at once a large handsome flower sprang up. It looked something like a tulip, but its leaves were as tightly closed as if they were the leaves of a bud. "What a lovely flower!" said the woman, kissing its red and golden coloured leaves. At her kiss the leaves burst open with a crack and she saw that it was really a tulip such as one can see almost anywhere. But lo! in the very centre of the blossom, on one of the green velvet stamens, sat a tiny maiden, a delicate and graceful little creature, scarcely half as long as a thumb; and when the woman saw her she called her Thumbykin, because she was so small.

A finely polished walnut shell formed her cradle, and therein, on a bed of violets, under a roseleaf coverlet

Thumbykin slept soundly at night. During the day she amused herself by floating across a plate full of water in a large tulip-leaf which served her for a boat. The woman had placed the plate of water on a table, and put a wreath of flowers round the edge of it, and from side to side of the plate the little maiden rowed herself with two oars made of white horse-hair. It was pretty to see her and prettier still to hear her singing in a voice as clear as a tiny silver bell. Such singing certainly had never before been heard.

One night as she lay asleep in her pretty little bed, a large ugly old toad crept through a broken pane in the window and leapt up on the table. "What a lovely little creature this is!" she thought, "and what a charming wife she would make for my son!" So she took up the walnut shell in which the little maiden lay asleep under her coverlet of rose-leaf, and leapt with it through the window, and so hopped back again into the garden.

Now through the garden a broad stream flowed, and in its marshy banks the old toad lived with her son. He was uglier even than his mother, and when he saw the pretty little maiden in her beautiful bed he was able only in his harsh voice to cry, "Croak, croak, croak."

"Don't make such a noise," said the old toad, "or you will wake her and then she may fly away, for she is as light as thistledown. We will put her on one of the large water-lily leaves that grow in the middle of the stream. It will seem an island to her; she is so small. She will not be able to get away from it, and we shall have plenty of time to get the state-room under the marsh, where you are to live when you are married."

Out in the middle of the stream grew a number of waterlilies, with broad green leaves that floated on the top of the water. The largest of these leaves seemed much farther off than any of the rest, and thither the old toad swam, carrying with her the walnut shell in which Thumbykin still lay sound asleep.

Very early in the morning the poor little creature awoke, and when she saw where she was she began to cry bitterly, for all round the leaf on which she was there was water, and she could see no way of ever reaching the land.

Meanwhile, down in the marsh the old toad was as busy as possible decking out her room with sedge and yellow rushes, so as to make it pretty and comfortable for her new daughter-in-law. When she had finished her work she swam out with her ugly son to the leaf where she had placed poor Thumbykin. She wished to carry off the pretty bed that she might put it in the bridal chamber to be ready for the bride. To the little maiden the old toad in the water bowed low and said, "Here is my son. He is to be your husband, and you will have a very happy life together in the fine house I have prepared for you down in the marsh by the stream."

"Croak, croak, croak," was all the ugly son could say for himself.

So the old toad and her son took up the pretty little cradle and swam away with it, leaving Thumbykin sitting weeping all alone on the green lily-leaf. She could not bear to think of living all alone with the old toad, and of having her ugly son for a husband.

Now the little fishes, who had been swimming about in the water, and had seen the old toad and had heard every word she said, leaped up till their heads were above the water, so that they might see the little girl; and when they caught sight of her they saw that she was very pretty, and they felt very sorry that any one so pretty should have to go and live with the ugly toads.

"No, no!" said they. "Such a thing must never be allowed."

So all the little fishes gathered together in the water round the green stalk of the leaf on which the little maiden stood, and they bit the stalk with their teeth until at last they bit it through. Then away went the leaf sailing quickly down the stream, and carrying Thumbykin far away where the toad could never reach her.

Past many towns she sailed, and when the birds in the bushes saw her they sang, "What a lovely little girl!" On floated the leaf, carrying her farther and farther away, until at last she came to another land. Round her head a pretty little white butterfly kept constantly fluttering, till at last it settled on the leaf. He was greatly pleased with Thumbykin, and she was glad of it, for it was not possible now that the ugly toad could ever reach her, and the land through which she was sailing was very beautiful, and the sun shone on the water till it glowed and sparkled like silver. So Thumbykin took off her sash and tied one end of it round the butterfly, and fixed the other end to the leaf, which now sped on much faster than before, having the butterfly for a sail and took the little maiden with it.

Presently a great cockchafer flew past. The moment he caught sight of the maiden he seized her, putting his claws round her slim waist, and away he flew with her into a tree. But the green leaf floated on down the river, and the butterfly flew with it; for he was tied to the leaf, and could not get away.

Oh, how frightened Thumbykin was when the cockchafer flew away with her into the tree! She was sorry, too, for the pretty white butterfly which she had tied to the leaf; for, if he could not free himself, he would certainly die of hunger. But the cockchafer did not worry himself about that. He sat down beside her on one of the leaves of the tree, and gave her some honey from a flower to eat, and told her that she was very pretty, though not at all like a cockchafer. In a little all the cockchafers that lived in the tree came to visit her. They stared their hardest at Thumbykin, and one young lady cockchafer said, "Why, she has only two legs! How ugly that looks!" "She has no feelers," said another; "how stupid she must be!" "How slender her waist is!" said a third. "Pooh! she looks just like a human being."

"How ugly she is!" said all the lady cockchafers. Thumbykin was really very lovely, and the cockchafer who had carried her off thought so; but when they all said she was ugly, he began to think that it must be true. So he would have nothing more to say to Thumbykin, but told her that she might go where she pleased. Then the cockchafers flew down with her from the tree, and placed her on a daisy, and Thumbykin wept because she thought she was so ugly that the cockchafers would have nothing to say to her. And all the time she was in reality one of the loveliest creatures in the world, and as tender and delicate as a rose-leaf.

All the summer through poor Thumbykin lived all alone in the forest. She wove for herself a little bed with blades of grass, and she hung it up under a clover-leaf so that she might be sheltered from the rain. For food she sucked the honey from the flowers, and from the leaves every morning she drank the dew. So the summer and the autumn passed away, and then came the long cold winter. The birds that had sung to her so sweetly had all flown away; the trees had lost their leaves, and the flowers were withered. The great clover-leaf under whose shelter she had lived was now rolled together and shrivelled up, and nothing of it was left but a yellow withered stalk.

Poor Thumbykin felt very, very cold, for her clothes were torn, and she was such a frail, delicate little thing that she nearly died. The snow, too, began to fall, and each flake, as it fell on her, was like a whole shovelful falling on one of us; for we are tall, and she was only about an inch high. Then she rolled herself up in a dry leaf; but it cracked in the middle, and there was no warmth in it, so she shivered with cold. Very near the wood in which she had been living there was a large corn-field, but the corn had been cut long before this, and there was nothing left but the hard, dry stubble standing up out of the frozen ground. To Thumbykin, going through it, it was like struggling through another forest; and oh, how bitterly cold it was! At last she came to the door of the house of a field-mouse, who lived in a hole under the stubble. It was a warm, cosy house, and the mouse was very happy, for she had a whole roomful of corn, besides a kitchen and a fine dining-room. Poor little Thumbykin stood before the door of the house, just like a beggar girl, and prayed the mouse for a small bit of barley corn, because she was starving, having had nothing to eat for the last two days.

"Poor little thing" said the field-mouse, who was really a kind-hearted old creature, "come into my warm room and have dinner with me." The mouse was greatly pleased with Thumbykin, so she said, "If you like, you can spend the winter with me: of course you will keep my rooms tidy and tell me stories. I am very fond of hearing stories."

Thumbykin did all the kind old mouse asked her; and in return she was well treated and very comfortable. "We shall have a visitor soon," said the field-mouse to Thumbykin one day; "my neighbour pays me a visit once a week. He is much richer than I am; he has fine large rooms and wears a beautiful black velvet fur. If you could get him for a husband you would indeed be well off. He is blind though, poor man! So you must tell him some of your prettiest stories." But Thumbykin knew that the neighbour spoken of was only a mole, and she did not mean to trouble herself about him.

The mole however, came and paid his visit. He was dressed in his black velvet coat.

"He is very learned and very rich," whispered the old field-mouse to Thumbykin, "and his house is twenty times larger than mine."

Rich no doubt he was, and learned too; but never having seen the sun or the beautiful flowers, he always spoke slightingly regarding them. Thumbykin found that she had to sing to him; so she sang, "Lady-bird, lady-bird, fly away home", and "As I was going along, long, long", and other pretty songs, and the mole at once fell deeply in love with her because she had such a sweet voice; but being a prudent man, he said nothing about his feelings.

A short time before this visit, the mole had dug a long underground passage between the two houses, and he gave the field-mouse and Thumbykin permission to walk in this passage whenever they pleased. But he told them that there was a dead bird lying in the passage, and he begged them not to be frightened by it. "The bird," he said, "was perfect, with beak and feathers all complete. It could not have been dead long, and had been buried just where he had made the passage." Then the mole took a piece of rotten wood in his mouth, and it shone like fire in the darkness, and he went before them to light them through the long dark passage. When they came to where the dead bird lay the mole pushed his broad nose through the ceiling so as to make a hole.

The daylight fell through the hole and shone on the body of the dead swallow. Its pretty wings were closely folded, and its head and claws were hidden under its feathers. The poor bird had undoubtedly died of cold. It made the little girl very sad to see it, for she dearly loved the little birds. All the summer through they had chirped and sung to please her.

But the unfeeling mole thrust the swallow aside with

his crooked legs, and said, "He will sing no more now. What a wretched thing it must be to be born a bird. Thank Heaven, none of my children .will ever be birds. Birds can do nothing but cry 'Tweet, tweet!' and they always starve to death in the winter."

"Indeed, as a sensible man, you may well say so," cried the field-mouse. "What does his chirping and twittering do for a bird when the winter comes? Can his tweet, tweet, appease his hunger, or keep him from being frozen to death? And yet it is thought to be very well bred!" Thumbykin did not speak; but when the other two turned their backs on the dead bird, she stooped down and smoothed aside the feathers that covered the head, and kissed the closed eyelids.

"Perhaps it was you who sang so sweetly to me in the summer," she said; "and how much pleasure you gave me, you dear pretty bird!"

The mole then stopped up the hole through which the daylight came, and walked home with the ladies. But at night Thumbykin could not sleep; so she got out of bed, and wove a fine large rug of soft hay. When she had finished it, she gathered together some soft flower down that she found in the field-mouse's sitting-room; and she carried the rug and the down to the dead bird. The down was soft and warm like wool, and she put it carefully round him and spread the coverlet over him, that he might lie warm in the cold earth.

"Good-bye! you dear, pretty little bird," said she; "good-bye. Thank you for all the sweet songs you sang in the summer when the trees were green and the sun shone down warmly upon us." Saying this she laid her head on the breast of the bird, but almost at once she raised it in surprise. It seemed as if something inside the bird was going 'thump, thump'. It was the swallow's heart. The swallow had not been really dead but only numbed with the cold, and when the warmth again stole over him his life came back.

In Autumn all the swallows fly away into warm lands, and if one happens to linger too long, the cold strikes it, and it becomes frozen and falls down as if it were dead, and it lies where it falls and the cold snow covers it.

Thumbykin trembled with fear, for the bird seemed very large in comparison with a little thing like herself, only an inch long. But her pity was stronger than her fear, and being a brave little girl, she covered the poor swallow more thickly with the down, and ran and brought a balsam leaf that she herself had used as a coverlet and spread it over the bird's head.

Next night she again stole into the passage to see him. He was still alive, but he was very weak, and could only open his eyes to look for a moment at his kind little nurse, who stood over him, holding in her hand a rotten piece of wood, for she had no other light.

"Thank you, pretty little maiden," whispered the sick swallow; "I am so nice and warm now that I shall soon get back my strength, and be able to fly about again in the warm sunshine."

"Alas!" said she. "You must wait for some time. It is too cold out of doors just now, it snows and freezes. You must stay in your warm bed, and I will take care of you."

Then she brought him some water in a flower-leaf; and when he had drunk it he told her how he had wounded one of his wings in a thorn-bush and was not able to fly as fast as the other swallows; how they flew away without him; and how he fell senseless to the ground. He could not remember any more, and did not know how he came to be where he then lay. All the winter the swallow remained underground, and Thumbykin nursed him with the tenderest care. She did not say a word about the sick swallow to the mole or to the field-mouse, for they did not like birds. Soon the spring came, and the sun warmed the earth, and the swallow said good-bye to his kind little nurse. She opened the hole in the ceiling which the mole had made, and the glorious sunshine poured into the passage, and the swallow begged her to go away with him. "She could sit on his back," he said; "and he would fly away with her into the green woods." But the little maiden knew that it would vex the old field-mouse if she left her in that way, so she said, "No, I cannot come."

"Good-bye then, good-bye, you pretty little darling," said the swallow; and away he flew into the sunshine. Thumbykin gazed after him and tears filled her eyes. She dearly loved the pretty swallow, whose life she had saved.

"Joy, joy!" sang the bird as he flew away into the green woods. But poor Thumbykin was very sorrowful. She was not able to get out into the warm sunshine; for the corn which the farmer had sown in the field over the house of the field-mouse had grown up so high that it seemed a lofty and pathless wood to the little maiden who was only an inch high.

"Now," said the field-mouse to her one day, "you are going to be married, Thumbykin. My neighbour, the mole, has proposed for you. What a piece of luck for a poor girl like you! You must begin at once to get your wedding clothes ready. You must have both woollen and linen, for nothing must be wanting in the wedding outfit of a mole's bride."

Thumbykin had to set to work with the spindle, and the field-mouse hired four spiders who had to weave day and night. Every evening the mole came to pay his visit, and he always spoke of the time when the summer would be over. Then he said they would be married. Just now the sun was so hot that it burned up the ground and made it as hard as a stone. But the little maiden was not at all happy. She thought the mole tiresome and did not like him. In the morning when the sun rose, and in the evening when he set, she used to creep out at the door, and when the wind blew aside the ears of corn so that she could catch a glimpse of the blue sky, she used to think how lovely it was in the light, and long to see her dear swallow once more. But he never came back again, for by this time he had flown far, far away into the green woods. When the autumn came, Thumbykin had her wedding outfit quite ready; and the field-mouse said to her, "Well, Thumbykin, in a month now you shall be married." But the girl cried, and said she would never marry the tiresome mole.

"Nonsense, nonsense!" said the mouse. "Don't be foolish or I shall bite you with my white teeth. The mole will make you a very handsome husband. The Queen herself does not wear such a handsome black velvet coat. He has, besides, a full kitchen and cellar. You ought to be very thankful for your good fortune."

At length the wedding-day arrived. The mole came to fetch his bride. Thumbykin would have to go away and live with him deep under the earth, and never again see the warm sun because he did not like it. The poor little maid was very sad at the thought of saying farewell to the beautiful sun: and as the field-mouse had permitted her to stand at the door, she went out to look at it once more, and to say farewell to it.

"Farewell, dear bright sun" she cried, stretching out her arms towards it. Then she walked a little away from the house, for the corn had been cut, and there was only the dry stubble left in the fields. "Farewell, farewell!" she said again, throwing her arms round a little red flower that grew close beside her. "Give my love to the swallow, if you should ever see him again."

Suddenly a "Tweet, tweet" sounded over her head. She looked up, and there was the swallow himself flying past. As soon as he spied Thumbykin he flew to her with delight, and she told him her story, told him how unwilling she was to marry the stupid mole, and to live always under the earth, and never again see the bright sun. As she told him about her marriage she could not help weeping.

"The cold winter is coming now," said the swallow, "and I am going to fly away to a warmer land. Will you come with me? You can sit on my back. Tie yourself on with your girdle. Then we will fly far away from the ugly mole and his gloomy abode; fly far away over the hills to warmer lands—lands where the sunshine is brighter than it is here, where there are lovely flowers, and where it is always summer. Fly away with me now, dear little Thumbykin. You saved my life when I lay frozen in yonder black tunnel."

"Yes, I will come with you," said the little maiden. Then she sat down on the bird's back with her feet resting on his outspread wings; and she fastened her girdle to one of his stronger feathers. And the swallow rose high into the air, and flew fast over forest and lake, and over the snow-capped mountains. Poor Thumbykin would have been frozen, but she crept under the bird's warm feathers, peering out from time to time so that she might catch a glimpse of the beautiful lands over which they were passing. At last they reached the warm countries, where the sun shines much more brightly than it does here, and where the sky seems twice as high above the earth. There by the wayside and on the hedges there grew purple and green and white grapes, and pale lemons and golden oranges hung from the trees in the woods. The air was fragrant with the scent of myrtle and balm, and along the country lanes ran beautiful children, playing with large gay butterflies. The farther the swallow flew the more beautiful every place seemed to grow. At last they came to a lovely blue lake, and by the side of it, shaded by stately green trees, stood a pure white marble castle. It was an old building, and the vine leaves twined round its lofty columns. At the top of these there were many swallows' nests, and one of these was the nest of the swallow who carried Thumbykin.

"This is my house," said the swallow; "but it would not do for you to live here. Will you choose for yourself one of those beautiful flowers?—and I will put you down on it, and then you shall have everything you can wish to make you happy."

"That will be charming," cried the little maiden; and she clapped her tiny hands.

On the ground lay a large white marble pillar, which had fallen and been broken into three pieces. Between the pieces grew the most beautiful large white flowers. The swallow flew down with Thumbykin and set her on one of the broad leaves. But how surprised she was to see in the middle of the flower, a tiny little man as white and transparent as glass! On his head was a graceful golden crown, and at his shoulders a pair of delicate wings. He was not much larger than the little maid herself. He was the flower-elf. An elf-man and an elf-maid live in every flower, and this was the King of all the flower-elves.

"Oh, how beautiful he is!" whispered Thumbykin to the swallow.

The little flower-king was at first quite frightened at the bird. Compared to such a little thing as himself, it was a giant. But when he saw Thumbykin he was charmed. Never had he seen such a pretty girl. He took the gold crown from his head and placed it on hers; he asked her name, and begged her to marry him, and become as she should the Queen of all the flowers.

This was certainly a very different kind of husband to

the son of the toad or to the mole with his black velvet coat; so she said "yes" to this handsome prince, her new suitor. Then all the flowers opened, and out of each came a tiny lady and gentleman. They were all so graceful that it was a pleasure to look at them. They each brought Thumbykin a present; but the present she loved most of all was a pair of lovely white wings from a big white fly. When these were fastened to her shoulders she could fly from flower to flower.

Then there were great rejoicings, and the little swallow who sat in his nest overhead was asked to sing for them a wedding song. He sang as well as he could; but his heart was sad, for he was very fond of the little maiden, and had hoped never again to part from her.

"You must no longer be called Thumbykin," said the flower-elf to her. "It's an ugly name and you are very beautiful. We will call you Maia."

"Good-bye, good-bye," sang the swallow, sad at heart as he left the warm lands and flew away to the colder north. There he had a nest outside the window of a man who could tell fairy tales. For him the swallow sang "Tweet, tweet", and that's how we came to hear the whole story.

The Fir-Tree

Far away in the deep forest there once grew a pretty little Fir-Tree. The sun shone full upon him; the breezes played freely round him; and near him grew many other fir-trees, some older, some younger; but the little Fir-Tree was not happy, for he always longed to be tall like the others. He thought not of the warm sun and the fresh air; he cared not for the merry, prattling peasant children who came to the forest to look for strawberries and rasp-berries. Sometimes, after having filled their pitchers, or threaded the bright berries on a straw, they would sit down near the little Fir-Tree and say, "What a pretty little tree this is!" and then the Fir-Tree would feel more unhappy than ever.

"Oh that I were as tall as the other trees," sighed the little Fir, "then I should spread my branches on every side, and my top should look out over the wide world! The birds would build their nests among my branches, and when the wind blew I should bend my head so grandly, just as the others do!" He had no pleasure in the sunshine, in the song of the birds, or in the rosy clouds that sailed over him every morning and evening.

In winter, when the ground was covered with the white glistening snow, a hare would sometimes come scamper-ing along, and jump right over the little Tree's head; and then how miserable he felt! However, two winters passed away, and by the third the Tree was so tall that the hare was obliged to run round it. "Oh, if I could but grow and grow, and become tall and old!" thought the Tree. "That is the only thing in the world worth living for."

The wood-cutters came in the autumn and felled some of the largest of the trees. This happened every year, and our young Fir, who was by this time a good height, shuddered when he saw those grand trees fall with a crash to the earth. Their branches were then cut off the stems looked so terribly naked and lanky that they could hardly be recognized. They were laid one upon another in waggons, and horses drew them away, far, far away from the forest.

Where could they be going? What would happen to them? The Fir-Tree wished very much to know, so in the spring, when the swallows and the storks returned, he asked them if they knew where the felled trees had been taken.

The swallows knew nothing; but the stork looked thoughtful for a moment, then nodded his head and said, "Yes, I believe I have seen them! As I was flying from Egypt I met many ships; and they had fine new masts that smelt like fir. I have little doubt that they were the trees that you speak of. They were stately, very stately, I assure you!"

"Oh that I too were tall enough to sail upon the sea. Tell me what is this sea, and what does it look like?"

"That," said the stork, "would take too long!" and away he stalked.

"Rejoice in your youth!" said the sunbeams; "rejoice in your fresh youth, in the young life that is within you!"

And the wind kissed the Tree, and the dew wept tears over him, but the Fir-Tree did not understand them.

When Christmas drew near, many quite young trees were felled, some of them not so tall as the young Fir-Tree who was always longing to be away. These young trees were chosen for their beauty. Their branches were not cut off. They too were laid in a waggon, and horses drew them away from the forest. "Where are they going?" asked the Fir-Tree. "They are no taller than I; indeed, one of them is much less. Why do they keep all their branches? Where can they be going?"

"We know! We know!" twittered the sparrows. "We peeped through the windows in the town below! We know where they are gone. Oh, you cannot think what honour is done to them! We looked through the windows and saw them planted in a warm room, and decked out with such beautiful things: gilded apples, sweetmeats, playthings, and hundreds of bright candles!"

"And then?" asked the Fir-Tree, trembling in every branch; "and then? What happened then?"

"Oh, we saw no more. That was beautiful, beautiful beyond compare!"

"Is such a glorious lot to be mine?" cried the delighted Fir-Tree. "This is far better than sailing over the sea. How I long for the time. Oh that Christmas were come! I am now tall and have many branches, like those trees that were carried away last year. Oh that I were even now in the waggon! that I were in the warm room, honoured and adorned! and then—yes, then, something still better will happen, else why should they take the trouble

to decorate me? It must be that something still greater,
still more splendid, must happen—but what? Oh I suffer,
I suffer with longing! I know not what it is that I feel."

"Rejoice in our love!" said the air and the sunshine.
"Rejoice in your youth and your freedom!"

But rejoice he would not. He grew taller every day. In
winter and in summer he stood there clothed in green,
dark green foliage. The people that saw him said, "That
is a beautiful tree!" And next Christmas he was the first
that was felled. The axe cut through the wood and pith,
and the Tree fell to the earth with a deep groan. The pair
was so sharp he felt faint. He quite forgot to think of his
good fortune, he felt so sorry at having to leave his home
in the forest. He knew that he would never see again
those dear old comrades, or the little bushes and flowers
that had flourished under his shadow, perhaps not even
the birds Neither did he find the journey by any means
pleasant.

The Tree first came to himself when, in the courtyard
to which he had been taken with the other trees, he heard
a man say, "This is a splendid one, the very thing we
want!"

Then came two smartly-dressed servants, and carried
the Fir-Tree into a large and handsome drawing-room.
Pictures hung on the walls, and on the mantelpiece stood
large Chinese vases with lions on the lids. There were
rocking-chairs, silken sofas, tables covered with picture
books, and toys. The Fir-Tree was placed in a large tub
filled with sand; but no one could know that it was a tub,
for it was hung with green cloth and stood on a rich,

gaily coloured carpet. Oh, how the Tree trembled! What was to happen next? Some young ladies, helped by servants, began to adorn him. On some branches they hung little nets cut out of coloured paper, every net filled with sugar plums; from others gilded apples and walnuts were hung, looking just as if they had grown there; and hundreds of little wax tapers, red, blue, and white, were placed here and there among the branches. Dolls that looked almost like men and women—the Tree had never seen such things before—seemed dancing to and fro among the leaves, and high up, on the top of the tree, was fastened a large star of gold tinsel. This was indeed, splendid, splendid beyond compare.

"This evening," they said, "this evening it will be lighted up."

"Would that it were evening," thought the Tree. "Would that the lights were kindled, for then,—what will happen then? Will the trees come out of the forest to see me? Will the sparrows fly here and look in through the window-panes? Shall I stand here adorned both winter and summer?"

He thought much of it. He thought till he had barkache with longing, and barkaches with trees are as bad as headaches with us.

The candles were lighted—oh, what a blaze of splendour! The Tree trembled in all his branches so that a candle caught one of the twigs and set it on fire. "Oh dear!" cried the young ladies, and put it out at once.

So the Tree dared not tremble again: he was so fearful of losing any of his beautiful ornaments. He felt bewildered by all this glory and brightness. And now, all of a sudden, both folding-doors were flung open, and a troop of children rushed in as if they had a mind to jump over him; the older people followed more quietly. The little ones stood quite silent, but only for a moment. Then they shouted with delight. They shouted till the room rang again; they danced round the Tree, and one present after another was torn down.

"What are they doing?" thought the Tree. "What will happen now?" The candles burnt down to the branches, and as each burnt down it was put out. The children were given leave to strip the Tree. They threw themselves on him till all his branches creaked; and had he not been fastened with the gold star to the ceiling he would have been overturned.

The children danced about with their beautiful playthings. No one thought of the Tree any more except the old nurse. She came and peeped among the branches, but it was only to see if, perchance, a fig or an apple had been left among them.

"A story! a story!" cried the children, pulling a little, fat man towards the Tree. "It is pleasant to sit under the shade of green boughs," said he, sitting down; "besides, the tree may be benefited by hearing my story. But I shall only tell one tale. Would you like to hear about Ivedy Avedy? oi about Humpty Dumpty, who fell downstairs, and yet came to the throne and won the Princess?"

"Ivedy Avedy!" cried some; "Humpty Dumpty!" cried others. There was a great uproar. The Fir-Tree alone was silent, thinking to himself, "Ought I to make a noise as they do? or ought I to do nothing at all?" For he most certainly was one of the company, and had done all that had been required of him.

And the little fat, man told the story of Humpty Dumpty who fell downstairs, and yet came to the throne and won the Princess. And the children clapped their hands and called out for another; they wanted to hear the story of Ivedy Avedy also, but they did not get it. The Fir-Tree stood meanwhile quite silent and thoughtful; the birds in the forest had never related anything like this. "Humpty Dumpty fell downstairs, and yet was raised to the throne and won the Princess! Yes, yes, strange things come to pass in the world!" thought the Fir-Tree, who believed it must all be true, because such a pleasant man had told it. "Who knows but I, too, may fall downstairs and win a princess?" And he thought with delight of being next day again decked out with candles and playthings, gold and fruit. "Tomorrow I will not trouble," thought he. "I will thoroughly enjoy my splendour. Tomorrow I shall hear again the story of Humpty Dumpty, and perhaps also that about Ivedy Avedy." And the Tree mused upon this all night.

In the morning the maids came in. "Now begins my state anew!" thought the Tree. But they dragged him out of the room, up the stairs, and into a garret, and there thrust him into a dark corner where not a ray of light could enter. "What can be the meaning of this?" thought the Tree. "What am I to do here? What shall I hear in this place?" And he leant against the wall, and thought, and thought. And he had plenty of time for thinking it over;

for day after day and night after night passed away, and yet no one ever came into the room. At last somebody did come in, but it was only to push some old trunks into the corner. The Tree was now entirely hidden from sight and apparently quite forgotten.

"It is now winter," thought the Tree. "The ground is hard and covered with snow; they cannot plant me now, so I am to stay here in shelter till the spring. Men are so thoughtful! I only wish it were not so dark and so lonely!"

"Squeak! squeak!" cried a little mouse, just then gliding forward. Another followed; they snuffed about the Fir-Tree, and then slipped in and out among the branches.

"It is horribly cold!" said a little mouse; "or it would be quite comfortable here. Don't you think so, you old Fir-Tree?"

"I am not old," said the Fir-Tree; "there are many who are much older than I."

"How came you here?" asked the mice, "and what do you know?" They were most uncommonly inquisitive. "Tell us about the most delightful place on earth! Have you ever been there? Have you been into the store-room, where cheeses lie on the shelves, and hams hang from the ceiling; where one can dance over tallow candles; where one goes in thin and comes out fat?"

"I know nothing about that," said the Tree, "but I know the forest, where the sun shines and where the birds sing!" And then he spoke of his youth and its pleasures. The little mice had never heard anything like it before. They listened very closely and said, "Well, to be sure! How much you have seen! How happy you have been!"

"Happy!" said the Fir-Tree, in surprise, and he thought a moment over all that he had been saying,— "yes, on the whole those were pleasant times!" He then told them about the Christmas Eve when he had been dressed up with cakes and candles.

"Oh!" cried the little mice, "how happy you have been, you old Fir-Tree!"

"I am not old at all!" returned the Fir. "It was only this winter that I left the forest; I am just in the prime of life!"

"How well you can talk!" said the little mice, and the next night they came again and brought with them four other little mice, who wanted also to hear the Tree's history. And the more the Tree spoke of his youth in the forest, the more clearly he remembered it: "Yes," said he, "those were pleasant times! but they may come back, they may come back! Humpty Dumpty fell downstairs, and yet for all that he won the Princess; perhaps I, too, may win a princess!" And then the Fir thought of a pretty little delicate birch that grew in the forest, a real, and, to the Fir-Tree, a very lovely princess.

"Who's Humpty Dumpty?" asked the mice. In answer, the Fir told the tale. He could remember every word of it perfectly; and the little mice were ready to jump with joy. Next night more mice came; and on Sunday there came also two rats. The rats, however, did not find the story was at all amusing, and this annoyed the little mice, who, after hearing their opinion, could not like it so well either.

"Do you know only that one story?" asked the rats.

"Only that one!" answered the Tree. "I heard it on the

happiest evening of my life, though I did not then know how happy I was."

"It is a miserable story! Do you know none about pork and tallow? No store-room story?"

"No," said the Tree.

"Well, then, we have heard enough of it!" returned the rats, and they went away.

The mice, too, never came again. The Tree sighed, "It was pleasant when those busy little mice sat round me, listening to my words. Now that, too, is past! However, I shall have pleasure in remembering it, when I am taken from this place."

But when would that be? One morning people came, and routed out the lumber-room. The trunks were taken away: the Tree, too, was dragged out of the corner. They threw him on the floor, but one of the servants picked him up and carried him downstairs. Once more he beheld the light of day. "Now life begins again!" thought the Tree. He felt the fresh air, the warm sunbeams—he was out in the court. All happened so quickly that the Tree quite forgot to look at himself,—there was so much to look at all around. The court joined a garden. Everything was so fresh and blooming: roses so bright and so fragrant clustered round the trellis-work, the lime-trees were in full blossom, and the swallows flew backwards and forwards, twittering.

"I shall live! I shall live!" He was filled with delight and hope. He tried to spread out his branches; but alas! they were all dried up and yellow. He was thrown down on a heap of weeds and nettles. The star of gold tinsel that had been left on his crown now sparkled in the sunshine. Some children were playing in the court, the same merry youngsters who at Christmas-time had danced round the Tree. One of the youngest of them saw the gold star, and ran to tear it off.

"Look at this, still fastened to the ugly old Christmas Tree!" cried he, trampling upon the boughs till they broke under his boots.

And the Tree looked on the flowers of the garden now blooming in the freshness of their beauty; he looked upon himself, and he wished from his heart that he had been left to wither alone in the dark corner of the lumber-room. He called to mind his happy forest life, the merry Christmas Eve, and the little mice who had listened so eagerly when he related the story of Humpty Dumpty.

"Past, all past!" said the poor Tree. "Had I but been happy, as I might have been! Past, all past!"

And the servant came and cut the Tree into small pieces; heaped them up, and set fire to them. And the Tree groaned deeply, and every groan sounded like a little explosion. The children all ran up to the place and jumped about in front of the blaze. But at each of those heavy groans the Fir-Tree thought of a bright summer's day, of Christmas Eve, or of Humpty Dumpty, the only story that he knew and could tell. And at last the Tree was burned.

The boys played about in the court. On the bosom of the youngest sparkled the gold star that the Tree had worn on the happiest evening of his life; but that was past, and the Tree was past and the story also, past! past! for all stories must come to an end some time or other.

What the Old Man Does
Is Always Right

I'm going to tell you a story I heard when I was a little boy. Everytime I think about the story it seems better. Some stories are like some people—they improve with age.

Perhaps you have seen in the country an old farm-house with plants and moss growing on its thatched roof, and with swallows' nests under the eaves. The walls are sloping, and only one of the little windows can open. The branches of the elder-tree hang over the fence, and beneath it is a pool with a few ducks. There is a dog that barks at everything and everybody.

In that sort of house there once lived an old farmer and his old wife. They were poor, yet they had one thing that was no use to them—an old horse that got its food by grazing at the roadside. The farmer sometimes rode to town on it or lent it to a neighbour, who would do the old couple a favour in return. Still, it would have been a sensible plan to sell it or exchange it for something they really needed, but what should it be?

"You'll know best, old man," said the farmer's wife to him. "This is market-day; ride into town and either sell the horse or make a good exchange. Whatever you do I shall be satisfied. Off with you to market."

So she put his necktie on for him in a beautiful double bow, brushed his hat round and round with her hand, and gave him a kiss. Then off he went with the horse which was to be sold or exchanged.

The old man understood quite well what he was to do.

The sun was hot; not a cloud was in the sky; lots of people were walking or riding to market along the dusty road. There was no shade anywhere.

Amongst the crowd was a man leading a cow to market, as fine a cow as you ever saw.

"She must give lovely milk," thought the old man. "What a good exchange that would be—a cow for a horse!"

"Hullo, you with the cow!" he said. "What do you think of this? A horse is worth more than a cow, but I don't care; a cow would be more use to me. How would you like to exchange?"

"I'll gladly do that," said the man, so they exchanged.

The farmer might well have gone home then, for he had done what he set out to do, but as he had started for the market he went on, just for the sake of seeing it.

Presently, as he walked on with his cow, he came upon a man driving a sheep. It was a fine sheep, fat and with a thick fleece.

"I should very much like that," said the farmer. "It would find plenty of grass along our hedge, and in winter we could keep it in the kitchen. It would certainly be better to have a sheep than a cow."

"Shall we exchange?"

The man was quite willing, so now the farmer went on with a sheep.

Soon he noticed a man coming out of with a big goose

under his arm.

"Heavy, isn't it? A grand plump bird! How well it would look on our pond! My old woman would like it— it could eat scraps. She's often wished she had a goose, and here's the chance; she shall!"

"Shall we exchange? I'll be very glad to give you this sheep for that goose."

The other man had no objection, so our farmer now had a goose.

By this time he was quite near the town. The road was more crowded than ever with people and cattle; they were walking on the footpaths and even on a potato-patch at the roadside where there was a hen. It was tied by one leg so that if it got frightened it couldn't run away.

It had a bright eye and looked altogether a very clever fowl. "Cluck! Cluck!" it said; what it meant by that there is no knowing, but when our farmer saw it he said, "That's the finest fowl I've ever seen—finer even that the parson's broody hen. I really must have it. A fowl can always pick up food for itself. It would be a good bargain if I could get it for this goose."

"Will you exchange?" he asked the owner.

"Exchange? Not a bad idea."

So they did exchange.

The farmer had done a good deal on his way to town, and he was hot and tired, so when he came near an inn he thought he would have something to eat and drink. As he was going in he met a lad coming out carrying a sack filled with something.

"What have you got in that sack?" the farmer asked.

"Withered apples," answered the lad. "For the pigs."

"That's surely a waste. I wish my old woman at home could see them. Last year there was only one apple on our tree. It stood on our cupboard till it was useless. 'It's always property!' my old woman would say. Here she could see something like property—a whole sackful! Yes, I should like her to see that."

"What would you give for the sackful?" asked the lad.

"What would I give? This hen." So he handed over the hen, and went into the inn with his apples, putting them down by the stove. The stove was hot, but he didn't worry about that.

A lot of other people were there, horse-dealers and herdsmen, and two foreign travellers so rich that their pockets were almost bursting with money. And they could bet, as you will hear.

Suddenly there was a sound from the stove. The apples were frizzling.

"What's that?"

"Well, you see—" began the farmer, and he told the whole story.

"You'll catch it from your old woman, when you get home," said one of the foreigners.

"Not I!" said he. "She'll kiss me and say, 'Whatever the old man does is right!' "

"Let's have a bet on it. How much?"

"A sackful of money against my sack will be enough," said the farmer, "but I'll add my wife and myself for good measure."

"Fine! First-rate!" So the bet was made.

In a carriage belonging to the inn the farmer and the two foreigners drove back to his home.

"Good evening, old lady!"

"Good evening, old man!"

"I made the exchange!"

"Oh yes, you know your business!" said she, and gave him a hug, paying no heed either to the visitors or the sack.

"I exchanged the horse for a cow."

"Thank goodness! Now we shall have our own milk and butter and cheese."

"Oh, but I exchanged the cow for a sheep."

"All the better," said his wife. "You think of everything. We shall have sheep's milk and sheep's cheese and wool for stockings and coats. That is more than we could get from a cow, which would just keep losing its hair. Yes, you think of everything."

"But I exchanged the sheep for a goose."

"So we shall really have roast goose this year, you dear old thing! You're always thinking of something to give me pleasure. The goose can walk about and get fat before we roast it."

"But I exchanged the goose for a hen."

"A hen! What a good exchange!" his wife said again. "The fowl will lay eggs and hatch them, and soon we shall have a regular poultry farm. That's a thing I've always longed for."

"Yes, but I exchanged the hen for a sack of withered apples."

"What? I really must give you a kiss!" exclaimed his

wife. "My darling little husband! Let me tell you something. When you had gone this morning I began to think what I could give you for supper. An omelet with herbs? I've got eggs and I've got bacon, but no herbs. So I went over to the schoolmaster's. They've got herbs, but his wife is a mean thing though she does pretend to be so sweet. 'Can you lend me a handful of herbs?' I said. 'Lend?' said she. 'No, there's not a thing in our garden, not even a withered apple.' And now I could lend her a whole sackful! I could die of laughing!"

And with that she gave him a smacking kiss.

"I like that!" said the two travellers together. "Things go from bad to worse and they get cheerier! That's well worth our money."

So they handed over a sackfull of gold to the farmer who had been kissed instead of being scolded.

Yes, it always pays when a wife thinks and says that her husband knows best and always does the right thing.

That's my story. I heard it first when I was a child, and now you've heard it too and know that what the old man does is always right.

The Swineherd

There was once a poor Prince, who had a kingdom. His kingdom was small, but was still large enough to marry upon; and he wished to marry.

His name was known far and wide; and there were a hundred princesses who would each have answered "Yes!" and "Thank you kindly!" if he had asked her to be his wife; but he wished to marry the Emperor's daughter.

It happened that on the grave of the Prince's father there grew a rose-tree—a most beautiful rose-tree. It blossomed only once in every five years, and even then it bore only one rose—but what a rose! It was so sweet that whoever breathed its scent forgot all cares and sorrows.

And further, the Prince had a nightingale, who could sing as though all sweet melodies dwelt in her little throat. So he put the rose and the nightingale into silver caskets, and sent them to the Princess.

The Emperor had them brought into a large hall, where the Princess was playing at "Visiting" with her maids of honour; and when she saw the caskets with the presents, she clapped her hands for joy.

"Oh, I do hope it is a little pussy-cat!" said she—but the rose-tree with its beautiful flower was brought out.

"Oh, how prettily it is made!" said all the court ladies.

"It is more than pretty," said the Emperor; "it is charming!"

But the Princess touched it, and was almost ready to cry.

"Pah! papa," said she, "it is not made at all; it is natural!"

And all the court ladies said, "Pah! It's a natural rose."

"Let us see what is in the other casket, before we get into a bad humour," said the Emperor. So the nightingale came forth, and sang so delightfully that at first no one could say anything ill-humoured of her.

"*Superbe! charmant!*" cried the ladies; for they all used to chatter French, each one worse than her neighbour.

"How the bird reminds me of the musical-box that belonged to our blessed Empress!" said an old knight. "Oh yes! These are the same tones, the same phrasing."

"Yes! yes!" said the Emperor, and he wept at the remembrance.

"I do hope that it is not a real bird," said the Princess.

"Yes, it is a real bird," said those who had brought it.

"Well, then, let it fly," said the Princess; and she refused to see the Prince.

However, he was not to be discouraged. He daubed his face over brown and black, pulled his cap over his eyes, and knocked at the door.

"Good-day to my lord the Emperor!" said he. "Can I be taken into your service at the palace?"

"Why, yes," said the Emperor. "I want some one to take care of the pigs, for we have a great many of them."

So the Prince was made "Imperial Swineherd". He had a dirty little room close by the pig-sties; and there he sat the whole day, and worked. By the evening he had made a pretty little kitchen-pot with bells all round it. When the pot boiled, these bells tinkled in the most charming way, and played the old tune:

> *Ah! my dearest Augustine,*
> *All is gone, gone, gone!*

But what was still more curious, whoever held his finger in the steam of the kitchen-pot immediately smelt all the dishes that were cooking on every hearth in the city.

Now the Princess happened to walk that way; and when she heard the tune, she stood quite still, and seemed greatly pleased; for it was the only piece she knew, and she played it with one finger.

"Why, there is my piece!" said the Princess. "That swineherd must have been well educated! Go in and ask him the price of the instrument."

So one of the ladies ran in; but she drew on wooden slippers first.

"What will you take for the kitchen-pot?" said the lady.

"Ten kisses from the Princess," said the swineherd.

"He is an impudent fellow!" said the Princess when she heard this, and she walked on. But when she had gone a little way, the bells tinkled so prettily that she had to stop.

"Stay," said the Princess. "Ask him if he will have ten kisses from the ladies of my court."

"No, thank you!" said the swineherd; "ten kisses from the Princess, or I keep the kitchen-pot myself."

"That must not be either!" said the Princess; "but do you all stand before me that no one may see us."

So the court ladies placed themselves in front of her,

and spread out their dresses; the swineherd got ten kisses and the Princess—the kitchen-pot.

That was delightful! The pot was boiling the whole evening, and the whole of the following day. They knew perfectly well what was cooking at every fire throughout the city, from the chamberlain's to the cobbler's. The court ladies danced, and clapped their hands.

The swineherd let not a day pass without making something. One day he made a rattle which, when it was swung round, played all the waltzes and jig tunes that have ever been heard.

"Ah, that is *superbe*!" said the Princess when she passed by. "I have never heard prettier compositions! Go in and ask him the price of the instrument; but mind, he shall have no more kisses!"

"He will have a hundred kisses from the Princess!" said the lady who had been to ask.

"I think he is out of his senses!" said the Princess, and walked on; but when she had gone a little way, she stopped again. "One must encourage the fine arts," said she. "I am the Emperor's daughter. Tell him, he shall, as yesterday, have ten kisses from me, and may take the rest from the ladies of the court."

"Oh!—but we should not like that at all!" said they.

"What are you muttering?" asked the Princess. "If I can kiss him, surely you can!" So the ladies were obliged to go to him again.

"One hundred kisses from the Princess!" said he, "or I keep the rattle."

"Stand round us then!" said the Princess; and all the

ladies stood round them whilst the kissing was going on.

"What can be the reason for such a crowd close by the pig-sties?" said the Emperor, who happened just then to step out on the balcony. He rubbed his eyes and put on his spectacles. "They are the ladies of the court; I must go down and see what they are about!"

The ladies were so much taken up with counting the kisses that they did not notice the Emperor. He rose on his tiptoes.

"What is all this?" said he, when he saw what was going on; and he boxed the Princess's ears, just as the swineherd was taking the eighty-sixth kiss.

"Begone!" said the Emperor, for he was very angry; and both Princess and swineherd were thrust out of the city.

The Princess wept, the swineherd scolded, and the rain poured down.

"Alas! unhappy creature that I am!" said the Princess. "If I had but married the handsome young Prince! Ah, how unfortunate I am!"

The swineherd went behind a tree, washed the dirt from his face, threw off his old clothes, and stepped forth in all his princely robes; he looked so noble that the Princess could not help bowing before him.

"I have come to despise you," said he. "You would not have an honourable Prince! You could not prize the rose and the nightingale, but you were ready to kiss the swineherd for the sake of a trumpery plaything. You are rightly served."

He then went back to his own little kingdom, and shut

the door of his palace in her face. Now she might well sing:

> *Ah! my dearest Augustine,*
> *All is gone, gone, gone!*

Big Claus and Little Claus

There once lived in the same village two men bearing the same name. One of them had four horses, the other had only one; so to distinguish them from each other, the owner of four horses was called "Big Claus" and he who owned only one horse was known as "Little Claus."

All the week long Little Claus had to plough for Big Claus, and to lend him his one horse, and in return Big Claus lent him his four horses, but only for one day in the week, Sunday. Then Little Claus was a proud man, and smacked his whip over the five horses, all his for this one day at least. The people, dressed in their best, were walking to church, and as they passed they looked at Little Claus, ploughing with his five horses; and he was so pleased that he kept cracking his whip and crying out, "Hurrah! five fine horses, and all mine!"

"You must not say that," said Big Claus; "for only one of the horses is yours."

But Little Claus soon forgot, and when another party passed by, cried out again, "Hurrah! five fine horses, all mine!"

"Did not I tell you not to say that?" cried Big Claus very angrily. "If you say that again, I shall strike your one horse dead on the spot, and then there'll be an end to your boasting."

"Oh, but I'll never say it again, indeed I won't," said Little Claus, and he quite meant to keep his word. But presently more people came by, and when they nodded a friendly "Good-morning" to him, he was so delighted, and it seemed to him such a grand thing to have five horses to plough his bit field, that he flourished his whip and cried out, "Hurrah! five fine horses, every one of them mine!"

"I'll soon cure you of that!" cried Big Claus in a fury, and taking up a stone he flung it at the head of Little Claus's horse. So heavy was the stone that the poor creature fell down dead.

"Oh, now I have no horse at all!" cried Little Claus, weeping. But after a little he set to work to flay the dead horse, and he dried the skin thoroughly in the air. Then, putting the dried skin into a sack, he slung it across his shoulders, and set out to the nearest town to sell it. He had a long way to go, and had to pass through a large dark wood. Here a fierce storm burst forth, and the clouds, the rain, and the dark shaking firs, so bewildered poor Claus that he lost his way, and before he could find it night came down. Not far off stood a large farm-house. The shutters were closed, but Little Claus could see lights shining through the cracks at the top of the shutters. He went up to the house, and knocked at the door. The farmer's wife opened the door, but when she heard what he wanted she told him he must ask elsewhere. He couldn't come into her house; her husband was from home, and she couldn't let in a stranger in his absence.

"Well then, I must sleep outside," said Little Claus, as the farmer's wife shut the door in his face.

Near the farm-house stood a hay-stack, and between it

and the house was a little shed with a flat straw roof.

"I can sleep up there," thought Little Claus when he saw the roof. "It will make a capital bed, but I hope the stork may not take it into his head to fly down and bite my legs." For a stork had made his nest on the roof, and had mounted guard beside the nest, as wide-awake as could be, although it was night.

So Little Claus crept up on the roof of the shed, and there he turned and twisted about until he had made himself comfortable. The shutters he found did not close properly at the top, so that he could see all that went on in the room below. There he saw a large table spread with bread and wine, roast meat and fried fish. The farmer's wife and the sexton were sitting at table. She was pouring out a glass of wine for him, and he was eagerly helping himself to a large slice of fish—he happened to be particularly fond of fish. "It's really too bad of them to keep it all to themselves!" sighed Little Claus. "Oh, how I should like some!" and he crept as near to the window as he could. What a fine cake he could see now! Why, this was quite a feast!

Just then he heard the tramp of hoofs coming down the road to the farm-house. It was the farmer riding home.

The farmer was a real good-hearted fellow, but he had one strange weakness, he could not bear to see a sexton; the sight of one made him half mad. Now, the sexton of the neighbouring town was first cousin to the farmer's wife, and they were old playmates and good friends; so, knowing that the farmer would be from home this evening, he came to pay his cousin a visit; and the good woman, being pleased to see him, had put before him the best she had in her larder. Now, when she heard the tramp of the farmer's horse, she was frightened and bade the sexton creep into a large empty chest that stood in a corner. He did so, for he knew that the farmer would be almost wild if he came in and found a sexton in the room. The woman then hastened to hide the wine, and put the dishes inside her baking-oven, for fear her husband, if he saw the table spread with them, should ask for whom she had been preparing such a grand feast.

"Oh dear, oh dear!" sighed Little Claus on the top of the shed, when he saw the good things put out of sight.

"Anybody up there?" asked the farmer, on hearing the noise; and he looked up and saw Little Claus. "Why are you lying up there? Come down and come into the house with me."

So Little Claus came down and told the farmer how he had lost his way, and begged him for lodgings for the night.

"To be sure," said the good-natured man. "Come in quickly, and let's have something to eat."

The woman received them kindly, covered one end of the long table with a cloth and placed on it a large basin of porridge. The farmer was hungry and ate his porridge with a capital appetite, but Little Claus could not eat for thinking of the roast meat, the fish, the wine, and the nice cake that he had seen stowed away in the oven. He had put the sack containing the horse's skin under the table, and now, as he did not relish the porridge, he trod on the sack till the dry skin squeaked quite loud.

"Hush!" muttered Little Claus to his sack, at the same time treading on it again, so as to make it squeak even louder than before.

"What have you got in your sack?" asked the farmer.

"Oh! I've got a little conjurer there," replied Little Claus, "and he says we need not be eating porridge when he has conjured a feast of beef-steak, fried fish, and cake, into the oven on purpose for us."

"A conjurer did you say?" cried the farmer, and starting up he looked into the oven, and there, to be sure, were fish, and steak, and cake. They had been hidden there by the farmer's wife, and he thought it was the work of the conjurer under the table. The farmer's wife durst not say a word. Almost as bewildered as her husband, she set the food on the table, and the farmer and his guest began with a hearty appetite to eat of the good cheer.

Presently Little Claus trod on his sack again, and again the skin squeaked.

"What does your conjurer say now?" asked the farmer.

"He says," replied Little Claus, "that there are three bottles of wine for us standing just in the corner of the oven." So the woman was obliged to bring out the wine that she had hidden, and the farmer poured himself out a glass and enjoyed it. He thought it would be a fine thing to have such a capital conjurer as this.

"A proper conjurer this of yours!" said he at last. "Do you think he could conjure up the Evil One? I should rather like to see him."

"Of course," answered Little Claus; "my conjurer will

do anything I ask him.—That you will, won't you?" said he, again treading on his sack—"Didn't you hear him say 'Yes'?" he asked. "But I warn you he, the 'Evil One', is somewhat dark and unpleasant-looking, and you'll not like to see him!"

"Oh, I shall not be afraid. What will he look like?"

"Why, he is for all the world just like a sexton."

"A sexton!" said the farmer. "That is a pity! You know I cannot bear the sight of a sexton; but no matter, since I shall know that it is not a real sexton, I shall not care about it. Oh, I've plenty of courage, only don't let him come too near me!"

"Well, I'll ask my conjurer again," said Little Claus, and he trod on his skin till it went "squeak, squeak," and he bent down to listen.

"What does he say now?" asked the farmer.

"He says you must open the large chest that stands in the corner yonder. You have only to lift up the lid, and you will see the Evil One crouching down inside; but you must hold the lid firmly so that he cannot slip out."

"Will you help me to hold the lid?" said the farmer; and he went to the chest where his wife had hidden the real sexton, who sat huddled up, trembling, and holding his breath, lest he should be discovered.

The farmer raised the lid a little and peeped in. "Ugh!" cried he, springing back in affright, "I saw him; he is exactly like our sexton; oh, how horrible!"

Then he sat down at table again, and began to drink. The wine revived his courage; and neither he nor his guest ever thought of going to bed. There they sat, talking and feasting, till late in the night.

"Do you know," said the farmer at length, "I should like very much to have your conjurer; would you mind selling him to me? Name your own price; I don't care if I give you a whole bushel of money for it on the spot."

"How can you ask such a thing?" said Little Claus "He is such a useful and faithful servant. I would not dream of parting with him for his weight in gold ten times over."

"I can't offer you so much gold," said the farmer, "but all the same I should like very much to have him."

"Really," said Little Claus at length, "since you have been so kind as to give me lodgings for the night, I do not think I can refuse your request. I will let you have my conjurer for a bushel of money—only the bushel must be crammed full, you know."

"Certainly it shall," answered the farmer; "but you must take away the chest as well. I don't wish it to remain an hour longer in the house; it will always be reminding me of the hateful sexton-face I saw inside it."

So the bargain was struck, and Little Claus gave the farmer his sack, with the dry skin in it, and got for it a bushel of money. The farmer also gave him a wheel-barrow to carry away the money and the chest.

"Farewell!" said Little Claus, as he wheeled away in the wheel-barrow the money and the chest with the sexton hidden in it.

On one side of the wood flowed a broad, deep river. The stream was so strong that no one could swim against it, so a bridge had lately been built over it. Little Claus took his way over the bridge, but stopped in the middle of it, saying loud enough to be heard by the sexton in the chest, "Now, what on earth is the use of this great chest to me? It's as heavy as if it were filled with stones; and quite tires me out wheeling it along. I'll throw it out into the river: if it swims home after me, well and good; if not, it doesn't matter to me."

Then he took hold of the chest and lifted it as if intending to throw it into the water.

"Don't do that, I beg of you," cried the sexton from the inside of the chest; "please let me out first."

"Holloa!" cried Little Claus, pretending to be frightened; "is the chest bewitched? If so, the sooner it's out of my hands the better."

"Oh no, no, no," cried the sexton; "let me out, and I'll give you another whole bushel of money."

"Ah, that's quite another matter," said Little Claus; and he set down the chest, and lifted the lid; and out crept the sexton, greatly pleased at his escape. He kicked the empty chest into the water, and then took Little Claus to his house with him, where he gave him the bushel of money he had promised. So Little Claus had now a wheel-barrow full of money.

"I have certainly been well paid for my horse's skin," said he to himself, as he entered his own little room, and emptied his money in a heap on the floor. "How vexed Big Claus will be when he finds how rich my horse's skin has made me. But I shall not tell him exactly how it all came about." Then he sent a little boy to Big Claus to borrow a bushel-measure from him.

"What can he want with a bushel-measure, I wonder?"

thought Big Claus, and he cunningly smeared the bottom of the measure with clay, hoping that some of whatever was measured might stick to it. And so it happened. And when the measure was brought back to him, he found three silver coins sticking to the bottom. "Fine doings, upon my word!" cried Big Claus; and off he set to the house of his namesake, and demanded, "Where did you get so much money?"

"For my horse's skin, which I sold yesterday," was the answer.

"Are horses' skins so dear as that?" said Big Claus. "Who would have thought it?" And he ran home, took an axe, knocked all his four horses on the head with it, and then flayed off the skins, and took them into the town to sell. "Skins, skins, who will buy skins?" he cried as he went through the streets.

All the shoemakers and tanners in the town came running up to him, and asked what he wanted for them.

"A bushel of money for each," replied Big Claus.

"Are you mad?" said they. "Do you think we have money to spend by the bushel?"

"Skins, fresh skins, who will buy skins?" shouted he again; and still to all who asked how much he wanted for them he replied, "A bushel of money."

"The boor is trying to make fools of us," said some one at last in great wrath. Then the shoemakers took their straps and the tanners their leather aprons and they beat Big Claus.

"Skins, fresh skins, fine fresh skins," they mocked. "And let us mark his own skin till it is black and blue. Out of the town with the great ass!" So they thrust Big Claus out of the town.

"Little Claus shall pay for this," muttered he. "I'll beat him to death."

It so chanced that Little Claus's grandmother died that evening. She had always been cross and ill-natured to him but he felt really sorry. So he lifted the dead woman and laid her in his own warm bed, in hopes that the warmth might bring her to life again. For his own part he thought he could spend the night in a chair in a corner of the room as he had often done before. About midnight the door opened, and Big Claus came in with an axe in his hand. He knew where Little Claus's bed stood, so he went straight up to it, and struck the dead grandmother a violent blow on the head, thinking it was Little Claus.

"There's for you," cried he. "Now you'll never make a fool of me again." And off he went home.

"What a wicked man he is," sighed Little Claus. "So he wished to kill me. It was a good thing that grandmother was dead already, or that blow would have hurt her very much."

Then he dressed his grandmother in her Sunday clothes, borrowed a horse from a neighbour, yoked it to the cart, set his grandmother on the back seat so that she might not fall out when it was moving, and so drove away through the wood. At sunrise they came to a large inn, and there little Claus pulled up and went in to get something to eat. The landlord was a wealthy and a good man, but he was as quick-tempered as if he had been made of pepper and snuff.

"Good-morning!" said he to Little Claus. "You are early astir today."

"Yes!" said Little Claus. "I am going to the town with my grandmother; she is sitting at the back of the cart. But I cannot bring her into the room; will you, yourself, not take her a glass of mead? But you must speak very loud for she does not hear well."

"I'll do that," said the landlord, and he poured out a large glass of mead, and went out with it to the grandmother who was sitting bolt upright in the cart.

"Here is a glass of mead from your grandson," said the landlord. But the dead woman did not answer a word, but sat quite still.

"Don't you hear?" bawled the landlord as loudly as he could. "Here is a glass of mead from your grandson." Again and yet again he yelled the same thing, and as she did not stir he lost his temper and threw the glass of mead in her face. It struck her on the nose, and she fell backwards into the cart, for she was only seated upright behind and not fastened.

"What! what!" cried Little Claus, rushing from the inn and seizing the landlord by the throat. "You have killed my grandmother. See what a hole there is in her forehead."

"Oh, what a misfortune!" cried the landlord, wringing his hands. "All this comes of my hasty temper. Dear Little Claus, I will bury your grandmother as if she were my own, and I will give you a bushel of money, if you will only say nothing about this. If it is known they will cut off my head, and that will be very unpleasant."

So Little Claus got a bushel of money, and the landlord buried his grandmother as if she had been his own.

Then when Little Claus came home again with much money, he at once sent his boy again to Big Claus, asking him for the loan of a bushel-measure.

"What's this?" said Big Claus. "Did I not kill him outright? I must look into this myself." So he himself went across with the bushel-measure to Little Claus. "How did you come by all this money?" said he, his eyes almost starting out of his head, as he saw all the riches his neighbour had added.

"You murdered my grandmother instead of me," said Little Claus. "So I have sold her for a bushel of money."

"That's a good price, at any rate," said Big Claus. So he went home, took a hatchet and killed his own grandmother. Then he put her into a cart, drove to the town where an apothecary lived, and asked if he would buy a dead body.

"Who is it? And where did you get it?" asked the apothecary.

"It is my grandmother," answered Big Claus. "I have killed her, that I might get a bushel of money for her body."

"God protect us!" said the apothecary. "You are raving. If you say such things, you will have your head cut off." And then he talked to him seriously about the wickedness of what he had done, and told him that such a crime should certainly not go unpunished. He frightened Big Claus so much that he rushed out of the Surgery, leapt into the cart, whipped up his horse, and drove home.

The apothecary and all the people, thinking him mad, let him go where he would.

"You'll pay for this," said Big Claus as soon as he got into the main road. "Yes, you'll pay for this, Little Claus." So, as soon as he got home, he took the largest sack he could find and went across to Little Claus and said: "So, you have played me another trick. First I killed my horses, then my grandmother, and it is all your fault; but you shall no longer make a fool of me." Then he caught Little Claus and bundled him bodily into the sack, which he threw over his shoulders, saying, "Now, I am going to drown you."

But he had a long way to walk before he reached the river, and Little Claus was no light weight to carry. The road led past the church. The organ was playing, for the service had just begun. Among the congregation Big Claus saw a man to whom he wished to speak. "Little Claus cannot get out of the sack by himself," thought he, "and no one can help him, for all the people are in church. I shall just go in and call that man back into the porch for a minute." So he set down the sack and ran into church.

"Oh dear, oh dear!" sighed Little Claus in the sack as he turned and twisted in vain efforts to loosen the string with which the sack was tied. Just then a very old drover passed by. His hair was white as snow, and he had a stout staff in his hand with which he was driving a large herd of cows and bullocks before him, many more, indeed, than he, weak as he was, could manage. One of them knocked against the sack, and turned it over and over. "Ah, yes!" cried Little Claus, "I am still so young;

and I am soon going to heaven,"

"And I, poor fellow," said the old drover, "am already so old; and yet I cannot get there."

"Open the sack," said Little Claus. "Creep into it instead of me, and then in an instant you will be in heaven."

"Yes, with right good will I shall do so," said the old drover. And he opened the sack from which Little Claus sprang forth.

"Will you look after my cattle?" said the old drover as he crept into the sack; and Little Claus tied up the sack, and walked off with all the cows and bullocks.

Presently Big Claus came running back. He took up the sack, and flung it again across his shoulders. It seemed to have grown lighter, for the old drover was not half so heavy as Little Claus. "How much lighter the burden seems now," said he. "It must be because I have been hearing a psalm." So on he trudged to the river, which was deep and broad, and flung the sack with the old drover in it whom he thought to be Little Claus out into the water, and shouted after it, "There now, Little Claus, you shall never cheat me more!" He then turned homewards, but on passing a place where two roads crossed, whom should he meet but Little Claus with his cattle.

"How comes this?" said Big Claus. "Is it really you? Did not I drown you, then?"

"Yes," said Little Claus. "You threw me into the river half an hour ago."

"But how did you come by all these beautiful cattle?" asked Big Claus.

"These are sea-cattle," said Little Claus. "I'll tell you

the whole story. Thank you for drowning me; it has made me rich, really very rich. I was frightened when I lay in the sack, and the wind whistled in my ears when you threw me down from the bridge into the river. I sank to the bottom at once, but I was not hurt, for I fell on the softest, freshest grass. Immediately the sack opened, and the most beautiful little girl came towards me. She was dressed in white and wore a wreath of green leaves. She took me by the hand and said, 'So you are come, Little Claus! Here are some cattle of yours; and a mile farther up the road another and larger herd is grazing; I will give you that herd also.' Then I saw that the river was a sort of highway for the people of the sea, and that on it they walked and drove to and fro from the sea far up into the land where the river rises, and thence back to the sea again. No place can be more beautiful than the bottom of the river is. It is covered with the prettiest flowers and the sweetest, freshest grass. The fish swam past me as swiftly as the birds fly in the air; and what gaily-dressed people I saw there, and what fine cattle grazed on the hills and in the valleys!"

"Then why were you in such a hurry to come up again?" asked Big Claus; "if it was all so beautiful down there I don't think I'd have come back."

"Did not I tell you," said Little Claus, "that the sea-lady told me that a mile up the road—and by the road she could only mean the river, she can't come into our land roads—there was another and larger herd of cattle for me? But I knew that the river makes a great many turns, and I thought I'd save myself half a mile by taking the short cut across the land. So here I am, you see, and I shall soon get to my sea-cattle!"

"What a lucky fellow you are!" exclaimed Big Claus. "Don't you think that I might have some cattle too, if I went down to the bottom of the river?"

"How can I tell?" asked Little Claus.

"You envious scoundrel! You want to keep all the beautiful sea-cattle for yourself, I warrant!" cried Big Claus. "Either you will carry me to the water's edge, and throw me over, or I will kill you! Make your choice!"

"Oh, please don't be angry!" entreated Little Claus. "I cannot carry you in the sack to the river, you are too heavy for me; but if you will walk there yourself, and then creep into the sack, I will throw you over with all the pleasure in the world!"

"But if I find no sea-cattle, I shall kill you all the same when I come back, remember that!" said Big Claus.

They walked together to the river. As soon as the cattle saw the water, they ran on as fast as they could, eagerly crowding against each other, and all wanting to drink first.

"Only look at my sea-cattle!" said Little Claus. "See how they are longing to be at the bottom of the river."

"That's all very well," said Big Claus, "but you must help me first." And he quickly crept into a great sack which had lain stretched across the shoulders of one of the oxen. "Put a heavy stone in with me," said he, "else, perhaps, I shall not sink to the bottom."

"No fear of that!" replied Little Claus. However, he put a large stone into the sack, tied the strings, and pushed the sack into the water. Plump! there it fell straight to the bottom.

"I am much afraid he will not find his sea-cattle!" observed Little Claus, and he drove his own herd home to the village.

The Darning-needle

There was once a darning-needle who thought she was fine enough to be a sewing-needle."Take care to hold me firmly!" said the darning-needle to the fingers which picked her up. "Don't let me go! If you drop me, I'm so slender that it's doubtful if anybody could find me."

"That's all right," said the fingers, taking her round the middle.

"Notice that I have an attendant," said the darning-needle, drawing a long piece of thread after her.

The fingers were using the darning-needle to mend a pair of the cook's old slippers.

"This work is not good enough for me," said the darning-needle. "I shall never get through. I'm breaking! I'm breaking!"—and she broke. "Didn't I tell you I was too fine?"

"Now she's useless," thought the fingers, but they had to keep hold of her, for the cook made her a head out of sealing-wax and put her into the front of her dress.

"Well, I'm a brooch now!" said the darning-needle. "I was sure I should win respect. When one is really worth something, it is found out sooner or later." She smiled to herself—inside, for nobody can see from outside when a darning-needle is smiling!—and looked around as proudly as if she were riding in a coach.

"Are you made of gold?" asked a plain pin which was near her. "You look beautiful, and you have a head, though it is very small. Take care of it and see that it grows!"

This made the darning-needle so proud that she gave a jump—and jumped right out of the cook's dress into the sink.

"This is travelling," said the darning-needle, "but I do hope I shan't get lost." But lost she was. "I'm too fine for this world," she said, "but I have plenty of sense, which is always something," and she kept quite cheerful as she was carried down into the gutter.

All sorts of things were floating above her—shavings, straws and scraps of newspaper.

"How they hurry along!" said the darning-needle. "They don't know what is below them, but I'm here. There goes a shaving thinking of nothing in the world but itself. There's a straw spinning along—don't *you* think so much of yourself, you'll run into a stone! And there's a piece of newspaper; what was on it is forgotten, but how it spreads itself out!

"I'm quite content to stay here. I know what I really am, and here I mean to remain."

One day she saw something shiny lying near her. It was only a bit of broken glass, but the darning-needle thought it was a diamond, so when she spoke she pretended to be a brooch.

"Are you really a diamond?"

"Something of that kind."

So each thought the other was something valuable, and they talked about the conceit of others.

"I used to live in a case belonging to a young lady who was a cook," the darning-needle said. "She had five fingers on each hand, and oh, the conceit of them! Yet their work was just to lift me out of my case, and hold me and then put me back again."

"Did they shine?" asked the piece of glass.

"Shine! No," said the darning-needle, "but that didn't keep them from being conceited. All five on each hand were brothers, just fingers, and they stood proudly side by side though they were not all the same size. The outside one, the thumb, stuck out from the rest, and he had only one joint in his back, so he could just bow, but he said that nobody could get on without him. The one next him was always pointing at things—the sun, the moon— and he pressed down the pen when writing was to be done. The longest one could look over his head; next to him was one with a golden girdle, and the smallest—the Pinky—did nothing at all and was very proud of it. And between them, with their boasting, they let me drop into the sink."

"And so we sit here and shine!" said the bit of glass, and then a lot more water came pouring along the gutter and swept the glass away with it.

"He's off!" said the darning-needle, "and here am I still. I'm too fine, but I'm proud of it, and should be looked up to for it."

What wonderful thoughts she had! "I almost think I must be a sunbeam's child! Perhaps the sun is looking for me, here in the water. But I'm so slender that my mother could hardly see me. If my eye had not been broken off, I could cry—but I wouldn't; crying is not refined."

One day some poor children came and began to look in the gutter where they sometimes found old nails and even pennies. It wasn't a very nice way to play, but they enjoyed themselves!

"Oh!" cried one, who had pricked his finger with the darning-needle, "what a horrid thing!"

"I'm not a horrid thing! I'm a young lady!" said the darning-needle, but nobody heard her. Her sealing-wax had come off, and she was dull and dirty, but she thought that made her finer than ever.

"Here's an egg-shell sailing along!" cried the children, and they put the darning-needle into it.

"I'm black and this is white," said the darning-needle. "Black and white go very well together. People will see me properly now. If only I'm not sea-sick!"

Well, she wasn't sea-sick.

"It's a great help against sea-sickness to think you are no ordinnary person. The finer you are the more you can bear."

"Crack!" The wheel of a lorry had gone over the egg-shell.

"Oh! what a weight!" said the darning-needle. "Now I'm really sea-sick!"

But she wasn't though the lorry-wheel had gone right over her. She lay there all her length—and there let her lie.

The Emperor's New Clothes

Many years ago there was an Emperor who was so very fond of new clothes that he spent all his money on dress. He did not trouble himself in the least about his soldiers; nor did he care to go either to the theatre or to hunt, except for the occasion they gave him for showing off his new clothes. He had a different suit for each hour of the day; and as of any other king or emperor one is accustomed to say, "He is sitting in council," it was always said of him, "The Emperor is sitting in his wardrobe."

Time passed merrily in the large town that was his capital. Strangers arrived at the court every day. One day two rogues, calling themselves weavers, made their appearance. They gave out that they knew how to weave stuffs of the most beautiful colours and patterns, but that the clothes made from these had the wonderful property of remaining invisible to every one who was either stupid or unfit for the office he held.

"Those would indeed be splendid clothes!" thought the Emperor. "Had I such a suit, I might at once find out what men in my realms are unfit for their office, and be able to distinguish the wise from the foolish. This stuff must be woven for me immediately." And he caused large sums of money to be given to the weavers, that they might begin their work at once.

So the rogues set up two looms, and made a show of

working very busily, though in reality they had nothing at all on the looms. They asked for the finest silk and the purest gold thread; put both into their own knapsacks; and then continued their pretended work at the empty looms until late at night.

"I should like to know how the weavers are getting on with my cloth," thought the Emperor after some time. He was, however, rather nervous when he remembered that a stupid person, or one unfit for his office, would be unable to see the stuff. "To be sure," he thought, "I have nothing to risk in my own person; but yet I would prefer sending somebody else to bring me news about the weavers and their work, before I trouble myself in the affair." All the city had heard of the wonderful property the cloth was to possess, and all were anxious to learn how worthless and stupid their neighbours were.

"I will send my faithful old minister to the weavers," concluded the Emperor at last. "He will be best able to see how the cloth looks; for he is a man of sense, and no one can be better fitted for his post than he is."

So the faithful old minister went into the hall where the knaves were working with all their might at their empty looms. "What can be the meaning of this?" thought the old man, opening his eyes very wide. "I can't see the least bit of thread on the looms!" However, he did not speak aloud.

The rogues begged him most respectfully to be so good as to come nearer; and then asked whether the design pleased him, and whether the colours were not very beautiful, pointing at the same time to the empty frames. The poor old minister looked and looked; he could see nothing on the looms, for there was nothing there. "What!" thought he, "is it possible that I am silly? I have never thought so myself; and no one must know it now. Can it be that I am unfit for my office? It will never do for me to say that I could not see the stuff."

"Well, Sir Minister!" said one of the knaves, still pretending to work, "you do not say whether the stuff pleases you."

"Oh, it's very fine!" said the old minister, looking at the loom through his spectacles. "The pattern and the colours are wonderful. Yes, I will tell the Emperor without delay how very beautiful I think them."

"We are glad they please you," said the cheats; and then they named the different colours and described the pattern of the pretended stuff. The old minister paid close attention, that he must repeat to the Emperor what they said. Then the knaves asked for more silk and gold, saying it was needed to complete what they had begun. Of course, they put all that was given them into their knapsacks, and kept on as before working busily at their empty looms.

The Emperor now sent another officer of his court to see how the men were getting on, and to find out whether the cloth would soon be ready. It was just the same with him as with the first. He looked and looked, but could see nothing at all but the empty looms.

"Isn't it fine stuff?" asked the rogues. The minister said he thought it beautiful. Then they began as before, pointing out its beauties and talking of the patterns and colours that were not there.

"I certainly am not stupid," thought the officer. "It must be that I am not fit for my post. That seems absurd. However, no one shall know it." So he praised the stuff he could not see, and said he was delighted with both colours and patterns. "Indeed, your Majesty," said he to the Emperor when he gave his report, "the cloth is magnificent."

The whole city was talking of the splendid cloth that the Emperor was having woven at his own cost.

And now the Emperor thought he would like to see the cloth while it was still on the loom. Accompanied by a select number of officials, among whom were the two honest men who had already admired the cloth, he went to the cunning weavers who, when aware of the Emperor's approach, went on working more busily than ever, although they did not pass a single thread through the looms.

"Is it not absolutely magnificent?" said the two officers who had been there before. "If your Majesty will only be pleased to look at it! What a splendid design! What glorious colours!" And at the same time they pointed to the empty looms; for they thought that every one else could see the cloth.

"How is this?" said the Emperor to himself; "I can see nothing! Oh, this is dreadful! Am I a fool? Am I unfit to be an Emperor? That would be the worst thing that could happen to me.—Oh! the cloth is charming," said he aloud. "It has my complete approval." And he smiled most graciously, and looked closely at the empty looms; for on no account would he say that he could not see what two of the officers of his court had praised so much. All the retinue now looked and looked, but they could see nothing any more than the others. Nevertheless, they all exclaimed, "Oh, how beautiful!" and advised His Majesty to have some new clothes made from this splendid material for the approaching procession. "Magnificent! Charming! Excellent!" resounded on all sides; and every one seemed greatly pleased. The Emperor showed his satisfaction by making the rogues knights, and giving them the title of "Gentlemen Weavers to the Emperor".

The two rogues sat up the whole of the night before the day of the procession. They had sixteen candles burning, so that every one might see how hard they were working to finish the Emperor's new suit. They pretended to roll the cloth off the looms; they cut the air with great scissors, and sewed with needles without any thread in them. "See!" cried they at last; "the Emperor's new clothes are ready!"

And now the Emperor, with all the grandees of his court, came to the weavers. The rogues raised their arms, as if holding something up, and said, "Here are your Majesty's trousers! Here is the scarf! Here is the mantle! The whole suit is as light as a cobweb. You might fancy you had on nothing at all when dressed in it; that, however, is the great virtue of this fine cloth."

"Yes, indeed!" said all the courtiers, although not one of them could see anything; because there was nothing to be seen.

"If your Imperial Majesty will be graciously pleased to

take off your clothes, we will fit on the new suit in front of the large looking-glass," said the swindlers.

The Emperor accordingly took off his clothes, and the rogues pretended to put on him separately each article of his new suit, the Emperor turning round from side to side before the looking-glass.

"How splendid His Majesty looks in his new clothes! and how well they fit!" every one cried out. "What a design! What colours! These are indeed royal robes!"

"The attendants are waiting outside with the canopy which is to be borne over your Majesty in the procession," announced the chief master of the ceremonies.

"I am quite ready," answered the Emperor. "Do my new clothes fit well?" he asked, turning himself round again before the looking-glass as if he were carefully examining his handsome suit.

The lords of the bedchamber, who were to carry His Majesty's train, felt about on the ground, as if they were lifting up the ends of the mantle, and walked as if they were holding up a train; for they feared to show that they saw nothing and so be thought stupid or unfit for their office.

So in the midst of the procession the Emperor walked under his high canopy through the streets of his capital. And all the people standing by, and those at the windows, cried out, "Oh! how beautiful are our Emperor's new clothes! what a train there is to the mantle! wnd how gracefully the scarf hangs!" In short, no one would allow that he could not see those much-admired clothes; because, in doing so, he would have declared himself either a fool or unfit for his office. Certainly, none of the Emperor's previous suits had made such an impression as this.

"But the Emperor has nothing on at all!" said a little child.

"Listen to the voice of innocence!" exclaimed her father; and what the child had said was whispered from one to another.

"But he has on nothing at all!" at last cried out all the people. The Emperor was vexed, for he felt that the people were right; but he thought the procession must go on now. And the lords of the bedchamber took greater pains than ever to appear holding up a train, although, in reality, there was no train to hold.

The Garden of Flowers

There was once a young Prince who had so many and such beautiful books, that he could find in them anything he wished to know except where the Garden of Paradise was to be found, and this was just what he wished most to know.

When he was a very little boy, just beginning to go to school, his grandmother told him that every flower in the Garden of Paradise tasted like the sweetest of cakes, and that the stamens were full of the choicest wines. On one flower there grew history, on another geography, on a third tables; so that whoever ate the flower immediately knew his lesson; the more he ate, the more he learned of history, geography, or arithmetic.

At that time the young Prince believed it all; but when he grew bigger and wiser, and learned more, he saw plainly that the beauty of the Garden of Paradise must be something quite different. "Oh, why did Eve pluck the fiuit of the tree of knowledge of good and evil? and why did Adam eat of the forbidden fruit?" he kept thinking. "Had I been there it would not have happened, and so there would have been no sin in the world." Until he was seventeen years old, he kept constantly thinking about the Garden of Paradise.

One day he went into the wood; he went alone; for to wander thus was his chief delight.

The evening drew on, the clouds gathered, and the rain

poured down as if the sky were nothing but a vast waters-pout. It was as dark as it is at midnight in the deepest of wells. The Prince now slipped on the wet grass, now stumbled over the bare rocks that projected from the stony ground. Everything was dripping with water, and the poor Prince had not a dry thread on him. His strength was failing when he heard a strange rushing noise, and saw before him a large lighted cavern. In the middle of the cave a huge fire was burning, and a fine stag was being roasted before it. A woman, elderly but tall and strong, as if she were a man in disguise, sat by the fire, throwing upon it one piece of wood after another. "Come in," she said to the Prince; "sit down by the fire and dry your clothes."

"There is a great draught here," said the Prince, as he sat down on the ground.

"It will be still worse when my sons come home," answered the woman. "You are now in the Cavern of the Winds; my sons are the Four Winds. Do you understand?"

"Where are your sons?" asked the Prince.

"There is no use in answering stupid questions," said the woman. "My sons have plenty of work on hand; they are playing at ball with the clouds up there in the King's hall!" and she pointed upwards.

"Indeed!" said the Prince. "You speak more harshly, and are not so gentle as the woman I am used to."

"Yes, they have nothing else to do! I must be harsh if I am to keep my boys in order; and I can do it, though they are very headstrong. Do you see those four sacks hanging by the wall? They are as much afraid of them as you used to be of the switch behind the looking-glass. I bend them together, and then they must get into the sacks. They know they must obey, I can tell you. There they sit, and dare not try to come out till it pleases me. But here comes one of them!"

It was the North Wind. He brought icy coldness with him; large hailstones rattled on the floor, and flakes of snow flew all round him. He wore a jacket and trousers of bear's skin, a cap of seal's skin was drawn down over his ears; long icicles hung from his beard, and one hailstone after another fell from under the collar of his jacket.

"Don't go too near the fire," said the Prince; "you may get your face and hands frost-bitten."

"Frost-bitten!" laughed the North Wind. "Frost is my greatest delight! But what spindle-shanked boy are you, and how did you get into the Cavern of the Winds?"

"He is my guest," said the old woman; "and if you are not content with that explanation, you may go into the sack! Now, you know."

This was quite enough. The North Wind began to tell whence he came, and how he had spent the last month.

"I come from the Polar Seas," said he. "I have been on the Bear"s Island, along with the Russian whalers. I sat and slept at the helm of their ship when they sailed from the North Cape. Whenever I woke up I found the stormy petrels flying about my feet. They are strange birds. They give one flap with their wings and then hold them stretched out straight and fly away."

"Don't make such a story of it," said his mother. "Come to the point; what sort of place is Bear's Island?"

"That is a glorious place!" said the North Wind. "The ground seems made for dancing on, it is as smooth and flat as a plate. Half-melted snow partly covered with moss, sharp stones, and the skeletons of whales and polar bears are strewed over it, looking like the arrns and legs of giants, covered with musty green. You would fancy the sun had never shone there. I blew gently to clear away the clouds, and there I saw a little shed, built from the wood of a wreck, and covered with walrus skins with the fleshy side out. A living polar bear sat growling on the roof. I walked on the shore, peeped into birds' nests, looked at the poor naked young ones, who were crying with their beaks wide open; I blew into their little throats, and they learned to be quiet. Farther on the walruses with their swine-like heads, and teeth an ell long, rolled like gigantic worms beneath the waters.

"And now the fishery began; the harpoon was thrust into the breast of the sea-horse, and the blood spirted up like a fountain and streamed over the ice. Then I thought of my part of the sport. I began to blow, and set my ships, the icebergs, sailing to crush the boats. Oh! how the sailors screamed and shouted; but I screamed still louder. They were forced to unload their cargo, and to throw the dead walruses, and their chests, and the ship's cordage, out upon the ice. I shook snow-flakes over them, and left them in their crushed boats to drift south-wards, to taste sea-water. They will never come again to Bear's Island!"

"Then you have done mischief!" said the mother of the Winds.

"What good I have done, others may tell," said he. "But here comes my brother of the West. I love him the best of all: he smells of the sea, and has a right healthy coldness about him."

"Can that be little Zephyr?" asked the Prince.

"Yes, it is Zephyr," said the old woman; "but little he is no longer. In days of yore he was a pretty boy; but those times have long passed away."

He came in looking like a wild man, but he had on a sort of padded hat, that his head might not be hurt. In his hand he held a club of mahogany cut in the American forests, no trifling thing to carry.

"Whence come you?" asked the mother.

"From those forest wastes," said he, "where the thorny brambles weave hedges between the trees, where the water snake sleeps in the damp grass, and men seem to be unknown."

"What did you there?"

"I looked at the deep river, marked how it hurled itself from the rocks, and flew like dust towards the clouds, that it might give birth to the rainbow. I saw a buffalo swimming in the river; but the strong stream carried him down. A flock of wild geese were swimming there too. They flew up into the air when they neared the waterfall, leaving the buffalo to be hurled over it. That pleased me, so I raised such a storm as uprooted old trees and brought them to the ground with a crash, broken to splinters, or sent them careering down the stream."

"And have you done nothing else?" said the old woman.

"I have rushed wildly across the Savannahs; I have

stroked wild horses, and shaken the cocoa-nut trees. Yes, yes, I have many stories to tell! But we need not tell all we know. That you know well, don't you, old lady?" And he kissed his mother so roughly that she almost fell. He was a wild fellow.

Now came the South Wind in his turban and floating Bedouin mantle.

"It is very cold here," said he, as he threw wood upon the fire. "It is easy to see that the North Wind has arrived before me."

"Why, it's hot enough to roast a bear," said the North Wind.

"You're a bear yourself," said the South Wind.

"Do you wish, both of you, to go into the sack?" asked the old woman. "Sit down on that stone there and tell me where you have been."

"In Africa, mother," answered he. "I have been hunting lions in the land of the Kaffirs. Such beautiful grass grows on those plains, green as olives! There the ostrich ran races with me, but I was yet swifter than he. I came to the yellow sands of the desert. There one might fancy oneself at the bottom of the sea. I met with a caravan; they had just killed their last camel, in hopes of getting water to drink, but they did not find much. The sun was burning over their heads, the sands roasting beneath their feet. There seemed no end to the desert. I rolled myself up in the fine loose sand, and threw it up into the form of an immense pillar; a famous dance it had! You should have seen how frightened the dromedaries looked, and how the merchants drew their caftans over their heads.

They threw themselves down before me as they are wont to do before Allah. There they are all buried. A pyramid of sand stands over them. If I should one day blow it away, the sun will bleach their bones; and travellers will see that people have been there before them; otherwise, in such a desert, they might think it impossible."

"Then you have only done evil!" said the mother. "March into the sack!" And before he was aware of it, the South Wind was seized and popped into the sack, which rolled about on the floor until the mother sat down on it to keep it still.

"These boys of yours are desperately wild," said the Prince.

"Yes, indeed," answered she; "but I know how to make them obey. Here is the fourth."

Then in came the East Wind, dressed like a Chinaman.

"Oh! you come from the quarter, do you!" said the mother. "I thought you had been to the Garden of Paradise."

"I shall go there tomorrow," said the East Wind. "I have not been there for a hundred years. I now come from China, where I danced round the porcelain tower, till all the bells began to ring. In the street below there was an official flogging going on, and bamboos were being broken on the shoulders of people, from the first to the ninth rank, who cried out, "Thanks, thanks, my fatherly benefactor!" But the words came not from their hearts; so I rang the bells till they sounded, "Ding, ding, dong!" '

"You are a wild boy," said the mother. "It is well that

you go tomorrow to the Garden of Paradise. Your visits there always improve you. Remember to drink deeply there from the fountain of wisdom, and bring me home a flaskful."

"I will do so," said the East Wind. "But why have you put brother South into the sack? Let him come out. I want him to tell me all about the bird called the pheonix. The Princess, when I visit her once in a hundred years, always asks me about that bird. Open the sack, mother! and I will give you two cupfuls of tea, as fresh and green as when I plucked it."

"Well, then, for the sake of the tea, and because you are my darling, I will open the sack." She did so, and the South Wind crept out; but he looked quite ashamed because the stranger Prince had seen his disgrace.

"Here is a palm leaf for the Princess," said the South Wind; "it was given to me by the old pheonix, the only one in the world. He has scrawled on it, with his beak, his whole history during the hundred years of his life. The Princess can read for herself how the ph~nix set fire to his own nest; and sat therein and was burned like a Hindoo widow. How the dry branches crackled! How the smoke and steam rose from the burning nest! At last everything was consumed by the flames, the old phcenix was in ashes; but his egg lay glowing in the fire, it burst with a loud noise, and the young one flew out. He is now king over all the birds, and the only phoenix in the world. He has bitten a hole in the leaf I gave you; that is his greeting to the Princess."

"Well, now, let us have something to eat," said the

mother of the Winds; and accordingly they all sat down to partake of the roasted stag. The Prince sat next to the East Wind, and they soon became good friends.

"What Princess is that of whom you have been talking?" said the Prince, "and where is the Garden of Paradise?"

"Ha, ha!" said the East Wind, "do you wish to go there? Well, then, fly with me tomorrow; but I must tell you that no human being has been there since Adam and Eve's time. You have read of them in your Bible, I suppose?"

"Of course I have," answered the Prince.

"Well, when they were driven out of it, the Garden sank under the earth; but it still kept its warm sunshine, its balmy air, and all its beauty. The queen of the fairies makes it her abode, and there also is the Island of Bliss, where death never comes, and where life is so beautiful! I can take you there tomorrow if you seat yourself on my back. But don't talk any more now, for I wish to sleep." And then they all went to sleep.

When the Prince awoke in the morning, he was not a little astonished to find himself already far above the clouds. He was sitting on the back of the East Wind, who kept tight hold of him; and they flew so high that woods and meadows, rivers and seas, appeared like a large coloured map.

"Good-morning!" said the East Wind. "You may as well sleep a little longer, for there is not much to be seen in the flat country beneath us, unless you like to count the churches; they stand like little bits of challc on the green board there below." By the green board he meant the fields and meadows.

"It was rude of me not to say good-bye to your mother and brothers," said the Prince.

"They'll excuse you as you were asleep," said the East Wind. And now they flew on faster than ever. How fast, might be seen by the rustling of the trees as they passed them; by the waves rising higher on the seas and lakes as they crossed them; and by the large ships dipping down into the water like swans diving.

In the evening, when it became dark, the large towns had a most curious appearance. Lights were burning here and there; it was just like watching the sparks on a burnt piece of paper as they go out one after the other. The Prince clapped his hands; but the East Wind begged him to be quiet and to hold fast, as otherwise he might fall, and be left hanging from the top of a church steeple.

"Now you can see the Himalaya mountains," said the East Wind; "they are the highest in Asia. We shall soon come now to the Garden of Paradise." So they turned more towards the South, and soon inhaled the fragrance of spices and flowers. Figs and pomegranates were growing wild; blue and purple grapes hung from the vines. Here they descended and stretched themselves on the soft grass while the flowers nodded to the Wind, as if they wished to say, "Welcome, welcome!"

"Are we now in the Garden of Paradise?" asked the Prince.

"No, not yet," said the East Wind, "but we shall soon be there. Do you see yon rock, and the cavern beneath it, in front of which the vine branches hang like a large green curtain? We must go through that. Wrap your cloak about you; for though the sun scorches here, farther on and you will find it as cold as ice. The bird that is flying past the cave has one wing warm as summer, and the other as cold as winter."

"This, then, is the way to the Garden of Paradise!" said the Prince as they went into the cave. It was bitter cold; but the cold did not last long, for the East Wind spread out his wings and they shone like the purest flame. What a cavern it was! Large blocks of stone, from which water was trickling, hung in the strangest shapes above them. Sometimes it was so narrow that they had to creep along on their hands and knees, and at other times it was so lofty and wide, they might have been in the open air. It looked like a chapel for the dead with its silent organ turned to stone.

"Surely we are going through the Valley of Death, to reach the Garden of Paradise?" said the Prince; but the East Wind pointed without a word to where the loveliest blue light was beaming to meet them. The rocks above them grew like mists, and at last were as clear and bright as white clouds in the moonlight. The air was balmy, fresh as a breeze among the mountains, and fragrant as one blowing through a valley of roses. A river, as clear as the air itself, flowed at their feet. Gold and silver fish swam in it; purple eels, that emitted blue sparks at every motion, were playing beneath its surface, and the broad leaves of the water-lilies that floated upon it shone with all the colours of the rainbow. The glowing orange-coloured flower itself seemed to draw its nourishment from the water, as the flame of a lamp draws its nourishment from the oil. A bridge of marble, of such cunning workmanship that it seemed made of lace and pearl, led over the water to the Island of Bliss, where bloomed the Garden of Paradise. The East Wind carried the Prince over. The flowers and leaves sang the sweetest songs about his childhood, in tones so soft and full that no human voice could match them. Whether they were palm-trees or gigantic water-plants that grew here, the Prince knew not; but he had never before seen trees so large and full of sap; and hanging about them in long wreaths like the illuminations on the margins of old missals were the most singular creepers. Birds, flowers, and scrolls were mingled in the strangest confusion. Close to them, in the grass, stood a flock of peacocks, with their bright tails spread out. The Prince touched them, but found to his surprise that they were not birds but plants: they were plantain-leaves, that sparkled like the tails of peacocks. Lions and tigers, perfectly tame, sprang like cats over green hedges, from which there came a scent like that of the sweet-smelling flower of the olive. The timid woodturtle, her plumage bright as the loveliest pearl, flapped her wings against the lion's mane; and the shy antelope stood by, and nodded his head as if he too wished to play.

And now came the Fairy of Paradise. Her garments shone like the sun, and her face, like that of a happy mother rejoicing over her child, beamed with delight. She was young and beautiful, and a train of lovely maid-

ens followed her, each having a star sparkling in her hair.
The East Wind gave her the leaf of the pheonix, and her
eyes beamed with joy. She took the Prince by the hand,
and led him into her palace, the walls of which were
coloured like a tulip leaf when it is held towards the sun.
The roof was like a flower turned upside down, whose
cup appeared the deeper the longer you looked into it.
The Prince stepped to the window, and looked through
one of the panes, and there he saw what seemed to be the
tree of knowledge of good and evil, with the Serpent, and
Adam and Eve, standing beside it. "Were they not driven
out?" asked he. The Fairy smiled, and told him that Time
had marked each event on a window pane in the form of
a picture; but that these were not like common pictures,
for everything in them lived; the leaves of the trees moved,
and men came and went, as in a mirror. He looked through
another pane, and there saw Jacob's dream; the ladder
rose to Heaven, and angels with their large wings were
moving up and down. Yes, everything that had happened
in the world lived and moved in the panes of glass. Time
only could have made such cunning pictures.

The Fairy now led the Prince into a spacious hall, whose
walls seemed transparent and were covered with portraits,
each more lovely than another. There were millions of
blessed spirits, whose laughter and song made one sweet
melody. In the midst of the hall stood a large tree with
drooping branches. Golden apples, of different sizes, hung
like oranges among the green leaves. This was the tree of
knowledge of good and evil, of the fruit of which Adam
and Eve did eat. From every leaf there dropped a bright

red drop of dew, as though the tree wept tears of blood for our first parents' sin.

"Let us get into the boat," said the Fairy; "we shall find it refreshing. The boat is rocked on the swelling waves, without stirring from its place; and all the countries in the world appear to glide past." And it was indeed strange to see. First came the high, snow-covered Alps, with their clouds and dark fir-trees. The horn's deep tones were heard, as was the voice of the herdsman singing merrily in the valley below. Then the banyan-trees bent their long drooping branches over the boat, coal-black swans glided over the water, and the strangest-looking animals and flowers were to be seen on the distant shore. It was Australia, the fifth division of the world, that now glided by withblue mountains in the background. And now came the hymns of priests, the dance of savages, accompanied by the noise of drums and the clang of bone trumpets. Egypt's cloud-aspiring pyramids, overthrown pillars, and sphinxes sailed by. The northern lights flashed over the extinct volcanoes of the North, in fireworks such as no mortal could imitate. The Prince was so happy! He saw a hundred times more than we have related here.

"And may I stay here always?" asked he.

"That depends upon yourself," answered the Fairy. "If you do not, like Adam, do what is forbidden, you may stay here always."

"I will not touch the fruit of the tree of knowledge of good and evil," said the Prince; "there are a thousand fruits here quite as beautiful.

"Examine your own heart," said the Princess, "and if

you do not feel strong enough, return with the East Wind who brought you. He is just going to fly back, and he will not return for a hundred years. The time will pass away here as if it were only a hundred hours; but it is a long time for temptation and sin. Every evening when I leave you, I must invite you to "Come with me!" I must beckon to you, but—beware of attending to my call. Come not with me, for every step will but increase the temptation. You will come into the hall where the tree of knowledge of good and evil stands; I shall sleep among its fragrant hanging branches; you will bend over me, and if you touch me, Paradise will sink beneath the earth, and be lost to you. The sharp wind of the desert will whistle around, the cold rain will drip from your hair, sorrow and care will be your lot."

"I will stay here," said the Prince. And the East Wind kissed his forehead, and said: "Be strong, and we shall see each other again after a hundred years. Farewell, farewell!" Then he spread out his great wings which shone like lightning in harvest-time, or the northern lights in winter. "Farewell, farewell!" resounded from the trees and flowers. Storks and pelicans, like a long streaming ribbon, flew after him, accompanying him to the end of the garden.

"Now we will begin our dances," said the Fairy, "and when the sun is sinking, while I am dancing with you, you will see me beckon, you will hear me say, "Come with me". But do not follow. For a hundred years I must repeat this call to you every evening. Every day, if you resist, your strength will increase, till at last you will not even think of following. This evening will be the first time,—I have warned you!"

The Fairy then led him into a large hall, filled with white transparent lilies, whose yellow stamens formed little golden harps, sending forth clear, sweet tones resembling those of the flute.

The sun was setting; the whole sky was like pure gold; and the lilies shone amid the purple gleam, like the loveliest roses. The Prince saw the background of the hall opening, and there stood the tree of knowledge of good and evil in a splendour that dazzled his eyes. A song floated over him, sweet and gentle as his mother's voice. It seemed as though she said, "My child; my dear, dear child!"

Then the Fairy beckoned gracefully, saying, "Come with me, come with me!" and he rushed to her, forgetting his promise, even on this the first evening.

The fragrance, the spicy fragrance around, grew stronger; the harps sounded more sweetly; and it seemed as though the millions of smiling heads, in the hall where the tree of knowledge of good and evil was growing, nodded and sang, "Let us know everything! Man is lord of the earth!" And they were no longer tears of blood that dropped from the leaves of the tree of knowledge of good and evil; they were red sparkling stars—so it appeared to him.

"Come with me, come with me!" Thus spoke those trembling tones; and the Fairy bent the boughs asunder, and in another moment was hidden within them.

"I have not yet sinned," said the Prince, "neither will I."

He flung aside the boughs where she was sleeping—beautiful as only the Fairy of the Garden of Paradise could be. She smiled as she slept. He bent over her, and saw tears tremble behind her eyelashes. "Weepest thou for me?" whispered he. "Weep not, loveliest of beings!" Then he kissed the tears from her eyes; he kissed her lips. There was a fearfull clap of thunder, more loud and deep than any that had ever been heard. All things rushed together in wild confusion; the charming Fairy vanished; the blooming Paradise sank so low! so low! The Prince saw it sink amid the darkness of night; it shone in the distance like a little glimmering star. A deadly coldness shot through his limbs; his eyes closed and he lay for some time apparently dead.

The cold rain was beating on his face; the sharp wind was blowing upon his forehead, when the Prince's consciousness returned.

"What have I done?" said he. "I have sinned like Adam; I have sinned, and Paradise has sunk low, beneath the earth!" And he opened his eyes and saw the star in the distance, the star which sparkled like his lost Paradise. It was the morning star.

He stood upright, and found himself in the wood, near the Cavern of the Winds. The mother of the Winds sat by his side; she looked very angry, and raised her hand. "Already, on the first evening!" said she. "Truly I expected it. Well, if you were my son, you should go forthwith into the sack."

"He shall go there!" said Death. He was a strong old man, with a scythe in his hand, and with large black wings. "He shall be laid in the coffin, but not yet. I shall suffer him to wander a little while upon the earth to repent of his sin. He may improve, he may grow good. I shall return one day when he least expects it and lay him in the black coffin. If his head and heart are still full of sin, he will sink lower than the Garden of Paradise sank; but if he have become good and holy, I shall put the coffin on my head, and fly to the star yonder. The Garden of Paradise blooms there also; and he shall enter and remain in the star, that bright sparkling star, for ever!"

The Shepherdess and
the Chimney-sweep

Have you ever seen an old-fashioned oak cabinet, black with age and covered every inch of it with carved foliage and curious figures? Just such a cabinet, an heirloom once the property of its present mistress's great-grandmother, stood in a parlour. It was covered from top to bottom with carved roses and tulips, and little stags' heads with long branching antlers peered forth from the curious scrolls and foliage surrounding them. In the middle of the cabinet was carved the full-length figure of a man, who seemed to be perpetually grinning, perhaps at himself, for in truth he was a most ridiculous figure. He had crooked legs like a goat, small horns on his forehead, and a long beard. The children of the house used to call him "Field-Marshall-Major-General-Corporal-Sergeant Billy-goat's legs". This was a long, hard name, and not many figures, in wood or stone, could boast of such a title. There he stood, his eyes always fixed upon the table under the mirror; for on this table stood a pretty little porcelain shepherdess, her mantle gathered gracefully round her and fastened with a red rose. Her shoes and hat were gilt, her hand held a crook; she was a most charming figure. Close by her stood a little chimney-sweep as black as coal, and made like the shepherdess of porcelain. He was as clean and neat as any other china figure. Indeed, the manufacturer might just as well have made a prince of him as a chimney-sweep, for though elsewhere black as a coal, his face was as fresh and rosy as a girl's, which was certainly a mistake—it ought to have been black. With his ladder in his hand, he kept his place close by the little shepherdess. They had been put side by side from the first, had always remained on the same spot, and so had plighted their troth to each other. They suited each other for they were both young, both of the same kind of china, and both alike fragile and delicate.

Near them stood another figure three times as large as they were, and also made of porcelain. He was an old Chinese mandarin who could nod his head, and he declared that he was grandfather of the little shepherdess. He could not prove this, but he insisted that he had authority over her; and so, when "Field-Marshal-Major-General-Corporal-Sergeant Billy-goat's legs" made proposals to the little shepherdess, he nodded his head in token of his consent.

"Now you will have a husband," said the old mandarin to her, "who, I verily believe, is made of mahogany. You will be the wife of a Field-Marshall-Major-General-Corporal-Sergeant, of a man who has a whole cabinet full of silver plate, besides a store of no one knows what in the secret drawers."

"I will not go into that dismal cabinet," said the little shepherdess. "I have heard that he has eleven china wives already imprisoned there."

"Then you shall be the twelfth, and you will be in good company," said the Chinaman. "This very night, as soon as you hear a noise in the old cabinet you shall be married, as sure as I am a mandarin;" and then he nodded his head and fell asleep.

But the little shepherdess wept, and turned to her betrothed, the china chimney-sweep.

"I believe I must beg you," said she, "to go out with me into the wide world, for we cannot stay here."

"I will do everything you wish," said the chimney-sweep; "let us go at once. I think I can support you by my profession."

"If we could but get safely off the table!" sighed she. "I shall never be happy till we are really out in the world."

Then he comforted her, and showed her how to set her little foot on the carved edges and gilded foliage twining round the leg of the table. He helped her with his little ladder, and at last they reached the floor. But when they turned to look at the old cabinet, they saw that it was all astir: the carved stags were putting their little heads farther out, raising their antlers and moving their throats, whilst "Field-Marshall-Major-General-Corporal-Sergeant Billy-goat's legs" was jumping up and down and shouting to the old Chinese mandarin, "Look, they are running away! They are running away!" The runaways were dreadfully frightened, and jumped into an open drawer under the window-sill.

In this drawer there were three or four packs of cards, none of them complete, and also a little puppet-theatre which had been set up, as neatly as it could be. A play was then going on, and all the queens, whether of diamonds, hearts, clubs, or spades, sat in the front row fanning themselves with the flowers they held in their hands, while behind them stood the knaves, showing that they had each two heads, one above and one below, as most cards have. The play was about two persons who were crossed in love, and the shepherdess wept over it, for it was just like her own story.

"I cannot bear this!" said she. "Let us leave the drawer." But when they again got to the floor, on looking up at the table, they saw that the old Chinese mandarin was awake, and that his whole body was shaking to and fro with rage.

"Oh, the old mandarin is coming!" cried the little shepherdess, and down she fell on one knee in the greatest distress.

"A thought has struck me," said the chimney-sweep. "Let us creep into the large pot-pourri vase that stands in the corner; there we can rest upon roses and lavender, and throw salt in his eyes if he come near us."

"That will not do at all," said she; "for many years ago the mandarin was betrothed to the pot-pourri vase, and there is always a kindly feeling between people who have been so intimate as that. No there is no help for it; we must wander forth together into the wide world!"

"Have you indeed the courage to go with me into the wide world?" asked the chimney-sweep. Have you thought how large it is, and that we may never return?"

"I have," replied she.

The chimney-sweep looked fixedly at her, and when he saw that she was firm, he said, "My path leads through the chimney. Have you indeed the courage to creep with me through the stove, through the fire-box and up the pipe? I know the way well! We shall climb up so high that they cannot come near us, and at the top there is a hole that leads into the wide world."

He led her to the door of the stove.

"How black it looks!" sighed she, but she went on with him, through the fire-box and up the pipe, where it was dark, pitch dark.

"Now we are in the chimney," said he; "and look, what a lovely star shines over us."

And it really was a star, shining right down upon them, as if to show them the way. So they climbed and crawled; it was a fearful path, so dreadfully steep and seemingly endless, but the little sweep lifted her and held her, and showed her the best places to plant her tiny porcelain feet on, till at last they reached the edge of the chimney. There they sat down to rest for they were very tired.

The sky with all its stars was above them, and the town with all its roofs lay beneath them. They would see all round them far out into the wide world. The poor little shepherdess had never dreamt of anything like this; she leant her little head on the chimney-sweep's arm, and wept so bitterly that the gilding broke off from her waist-band.

"This is too much!" she cried. "The world is all too large! Oh that I were once more upon the little table under the mirror! I shall never be happy till I am there again. I have followed you into the wide world; surely if you love me you can follow me home again."

The chimney-sweep talked sensibly to her, reminding her of the old mandarin and "Field-Marshall-Major-General-Corporal-Sergeant Billy-goat's legs". But she wept so bitterly, and kissed her little chimney-sweep so fondly, that at last he could not but yield to her request, foolish as it was.

So with great trouble they crawled down the chimney, crept through the pipe and through the fire-box and into the dark stove. They lurked for a little behind the door, listening, before they would venture to return into the room. Everything was quite still. They peeped out. Alas! on the floor lay the old mandarin. In trying to follow the runaways, he had jumped down from the table and had broken into three pieces. His head lay shaking in a corner. "The Field-Marshall-Major-General-Corporal-Sergeant Billy-goat's legs" stood where he had always stood, thinking over what had happened.

"Oh, how shocking!" exclaimed the little shepherdess. "My old grandfather is broken in pieces, and it is all our fault! I shall never get over it!" and she wrung her little hands.

"He can be put together again," said the chimney-sweep. "He can very easily be put together; only don't be so impatient! If they glue his back together, and put a strong rivet in his neck, then he will be as good as new, and will be able to say plenty of unpleasant things to us."

"Do you really think so?" asked she. And then they climbed up the table to the place where they had stood before.

"Well, we're not much farther on," said the chimney-sweep; "we might have spared ourselves all the trouble."

"If we could but have old grandfather put together!"

said the shepherdess. "Will it cost very much?"

He was put together. The family had his back glued and his neck riveted. He was as good as new, but could no longer nod his head.

"We have certainly grown very proud since we were broken in pieces," said Field-Marshall-Major-General-Corporal-Sergeant Billy-goat's legs, "but I must say, for my part, I do not see that there is anything to be proud of. Am I to have her or am I not? Just answer me that!"

The chimney-sweep and the little shepherdess looked imploringly at the old mandarin; they were so afraid lest he should nod. But nod he could not, and it was disagreeable to him to have to tell a stranger that he had a rivet in his neck. So the young porcelain people were left together, and they blessed the grandfather's rivet, and loved each other till they broke in pieces.

The Wild Swans

Far, far away, in the land to which the swallows fly in our winter-time, there dwelt a King who had eleven sons and one daughter, named Elise. The eleven brothers were Princes, and went to school with stars on their breasts and swords by their sides; they wrote on golden copy-books with diamond pens, and learnt by heart just as they read. In short, it was easy to see that they were Princes. Their sister Elise used to sit upon a little glass stool, and had a picture-book which had cost the half of a kingdom. Oh, the children were so happy! But happy they were not to remain always.

Their father, who was the King of the whole country, married a wicked Queen who was not at all kind to the poor children. They found this out on the first day after the marriage. There were great festivities at the palace; and the children played at receiving company, but, instead of letting them have, as usual, as many cakes and burnt apples as were left, the Queen gave them only some sand in a teacup, and told them to play at make-believe with that.

The week after, she sent the little Elise to be brought up by some peasants in the country, and before long she told the King so many falsehoods about the poor Princes, that he would have nothing more to do with them.

"Away, out into the world, and take care of yourselves," said the wicked Queen; "fly away in the form of great speechless birds." But she could not make them ugly, as she wished to do, for they were changed into eleven white Swans. Sending forth a strange cry, they flew out of the palace windows, over the park and over the wood.

It was still early in the morning when they passed the peasant's cottage where Elise lay sleeping. They hovered over the roof, stretched their long necks, and flapped their wings; but no one either heard or saw them, so they were forced to fly away. They flew up to the clouds and out into the wide world, far away into the dark forest, which stretched as far as the seashore.

Poor little Elise stood in the peasant's cottage, playing with a green leaf, for she had no other plaything. She pricked a hole in the leaf and peeped through it at the sun, and then she fancied she saw her brothers' bright eyes and whenever the warm sunbeams shone full upon her cheeks, she thought of her brothers' kisses.

One day was just like another. When the wind blew through the thick hedge of rose-trees in front of the house, she would whisper to the roses, "Who is more beautiful than you?" And the roses would shake their heads and say, "Elise." And when the peasant's wife sat on Sundays at the door of her cottage reading her hymn-book, the wind would rustle the leaves and say to the book, "Who is more pious than you?" And the hymn-book would answer, "Elise." And what the roses and the hymn-book said, was no more the truth.

When she was fifteen years old she had to go home, and when the Queen saw how beautiful she was, she hated her more than ever, and would willingly have turned her, like her brothers, into a Wild Swan; but she dared not do so, because the King wished to see his daughter.

Early one morning the Queen went into the bathroom which was made of marble, and fitted up with soft pillows and the gayest carpets. She took three toads with her and kissed them, and said to one, "When Elise comes to the bath settle thou upon her head that she may become dull and sleepy like thee. "Settle thou upon her forehead," said she to another, "and let her become ugly like thee, so that her father may not know her again." And "Do thou place thyself upon her bosom," whispered she to the third, "that her heart may become evil, and a torment to herself." She then put the toads into clear water, which immediately turned green, and having called Elise, took off her clothes and made her get into the bath. As she dipped her head under the water, one toad settled among her hair, another on her forehead, and the third upon her bosom. But Elise seemed not at all aware of it; and when she rose up three poppies were seen swimming on the water. Had not the animals been poisonous and kissed by a witch, they would have been changed into roses because they had rested on Elise's head and heart. She was too good for magic to have any power over her.

When the Queen perceived this, she rubbed walnut juice all over the maiden's skin, so that it became quite swarthy, smeared a nasty salve over her lovely face, and entangled her long thick hair, till it was impossible to recognize the beautiful Elise. When her father saw her, he was shocked, and said she could not be his daughter. No one knew her but the mastiff and the swallows; and they were only poor animals and could not say anything.

Poor Elise wept, and thought of her eleven brothers who were all away. In great distress she stole away and wandered the whole day over fields and marshes, till she came to the great forest. She knew not where to go, but she was so sad, and longed so much to see her brothers, who like herself had been driven out into the world, that she made up her mind to seek for them and find them.

She had not been long in the forest when night came on, and she lost her way amid the darkness. So she lay down on the soft moss, said her evening prayer, and leaned her head against the trunk of a tree. It was very still in the forest; the air was mild, and from the grass and mould around gleamed the green lights of many hundred glow-worms; and when Elise touched one of the branches hanging over her, bright insects fell down upon her like falling stars.

All the night long she dreamed of her brothers. It seemed to her that they were all children again, played together, wrote with diamond pens upon golden copybooks, and looked at the pictures in the beautiful book that had cost half of a kingdom. But they did not as formerly make straight strokes and pot-hooks upon the copy-books. No; they wrote of the noble deeds they had done, and the strange things they had seen. In the picture-book, too everything seemed alive; the birds sang, and the men and women stepped from the pages and talked to Elise and her brothers, jumping back into their places, however, when she turned over the leaves, so that the pictures did not get confused.

When Elise awoke, the sun was already high in the heavens. She could not see it, for the tall trees twined their thickly-leaved branches so closely together that, as the sunbeams played upon them, they looked like a golden veil waving to and fro. The air was fragrant, and the birds almost perched upon Elise's shoulders. She heard the noise of water, and when she went towards it she found a pool formed by several springs, with the prettiest pebbles at the bottom. Bushes were growing thickly round, but the deer had trodden a broad path through them, and by this path Elise went down to the water's edge. The water was so clear that had not the boughs and bushes around been moved to and fro by the wind she might have fancied they were painted upon the smooth surface, so distinctly was each little leaf mirrored upon it, whether glowing in the sunlight or lying in the shade.

When Elise saw her own face in the water she was frightened, so brown and ugly did it look; but when she wetted her little hand, and rubbed her brow and eyes, the white skin again appeared. So she took off her clothes, stepped into the fresh water and bathed herself, and in the whole world there was not a king's daughter more beautiful than she then appeared.

After she had again dressed herself, and had braided her long hair, she went to the bubbling spring, caught some water in the hollow of her hand and drank it, and then wandered farther into the forest. She knew not where she was going, but she thought of her brothers, and of the good God who, she felt, would never forsake her. He it was who made the wild apples grow to feed the hungry, and who showed her a tree whose boughs bent under the weight of their fruit. She made her noonday meal under the shade of this tree, then propped up the boughs, and walked on into the gloomiest depths of the forest. It was so still that she could hear her own footsteps, and the rustling of each little withered leaf that was crushed beneath her feet. Not a bird was to be seen, not a sunbeam penetrated the thick foliage; and the tall stems of the trees stood so close together, that when she looked straight before her she seemed enclosed by trellis-work upon trellis-work. Oh! there was a solitariness in this forest such as Elise had never known before.

And the night was so dark! not a single glow-worm sent forth its light from the moss. Sorrowfully she lay down to sleep. Then it seemed to her as though the boughs above her opened, and she saw the angel of God smiling down upon her, and a thousand little cherubs all around him. When she awoke in the morning she could not tell whether this was a dream, or whether it had really happened.

She walked on a little farther, and met an old woman with a basket full of berries. The old woman gave her some of the berries, and Elise asked if she had not seen eleven Princes ride through the wood.

"No," said the old woman, "but I saw yesterday eleven Swans with golden crowns on their heads swim down the brook near here."

Then she led Elise on a little farther to a sloping bank at the foot of which ran a little brook. The trees on each side stretched their long leafy branches towards each other, and where they could not unite naturally the roots had torn themselves from the earth, so that the branches might mingle their foliage as they hung over the water.

Elise bade the old woman farewell, and wandered by the side of the stream till she came to the place where it reached the open sea.

The great, the beautiful sea lay before the maiden's eyes, but not a ship, not a boat was to be seen. How was she to go on? She noticed how the numberless little stones on the shore had all been washed into a round form by the waves; glass, iron, stone, everything that lay scattered there had been moulded into shape, and yet the water which had done this was much softer than Elise's delicate little hand.

"The water rolls on unweariedly," said she, "till it smooths all that is hard; I will be no less unwearied! Thank you for the lesson you have given me, ye bright rolling waves; some day, my heart tells me, you shall carry me to my dear brothers!"

Upon the wet sea-grass lay eleven white swan-feathers. Elise gathered them up and put them together. Drops of water hung about them, whether dew or tears she could not tell. She was quite alone on the seashore, but she did not mind that, for the sea was full of interest to her; it was always moving, always changing, always new, and so gave her more pleasure in a few hours than the gentle inland waters could have given in a whole year. When a black cloud passed over the sky, it seemed as if the sea would say, "I too can look dark"; and then the wind would blow and the waves fling out their white foam; but when the clouds shone with a bright red tint, and the winds were asleep, the sea became like a rose-leaf now green, now white. Yet however smooth its glassy surface was, there was always a slight motion near the shore as the waves rose and fell like the breast of a sleeping child.

At sunset Elise saw eleven Wild Swans with golden crowns on their heads fly towards the land; they flew one behind another, looking like a long white ribbon. Elise climbed the slope from the shore and hid herself behind a bush. The Swans came down close to her, and flapped their long white wings.

As the sun sank beneath the water, the Swans' feathers fell off, and beside her stood eleven handsome Princes, her brothers. She uttered a loud cry, for although they were very much changed, Elise knew and felt that they must be her brothers. Then she threw herself into their arms, calling them by their names, and the Princes were very happy to see their sister, now grown so tall and so beautiful! They laughed and wept, and soon told each other how wickedly their step-mother had acted towards them.

"We brothers," said the eldest, "fly or swim as long as the sun is in the sky, but when it sets we appear again in our human form; we are therefore bound to look out for a safe resting-place before sunset, for if we were flying among the clouds at the time we should fall down into the sea when we recovered our human shape. We do not dwell here. A land quite as beautiful as this lies on the other side of the sea, but it is far off. To reach it we have to cross the deep waters, and there is no island midway on which we may rest at night. One little solitary rock rises from the waves, and upon it we only find room enough to stand side by side. There we spend the night in our human form; and when the sea is rough the foam dashes over us. But we thank God even for this rock, for without it we should never be able to visit our dear native country. Only once in the year are we allowed to make this visit to our home. We require two of the longest days for our flight, and can remain here only eleven days, during which time we fly over the large forest, whence we can see the palace in which we were born, where our father dwells, and the tower of the church in which our mother was buried. Here even the trees and bushes seem of kin to us. The wild horses still race over the plain as in the days of our childhood. The charcoal-burner still sings the same old tunes to which we used to dance in our youth. This is our fatherland to which we are drawn by ties of love; and here we have found thee, thou dear little sister! We have yet two days longer to stay here, and then we must fly over the sea to a land beautiful indeed, but not our fatherland. How shall we take thee with us? we have neither ship nor boat!"

"How can I break this spell?" said the sister. And so they went on talking almost the whole of the night. They slept only a few hours.

Elise was awakened by the rustling of wings, and saw the Swans fluttering above her. Her brothers were again changed into Swans. For some time they flew round in wider and wider circles, till at last they flew far away. One of them remained behind; it was the youngest. He laid his head in her lap and she stroked his white wings; they remained the whole day together. Towards evening the others came back, and when the sun was set, again they stood on the firm ground in their natural form.

"Tomorrow we shall fly away," they said, "and may not return for a year, but we cannot leave you here. Have you courage to go with us? Our arms are strong enough to bear you through the forest, and will not our wings be strong enough to fly with you over the sea?"

"Yes, take me with you," said Elise.

They spent the whole night in weaving a mat of the pliant willow bark and the tough rushes, and their mat was thick and strong. Elise lay down upon it, and when the sun had risen, and the brothers had been turned again into Wild Swans, they seized the mat with their beaks and flew up high among the clouds with their dear sister. She was still sleeping, and, as the sunbeams shone full upon her face, one of the Swans flew over her head and shaded her with his broad wings.

They were already far from land when Elise awoke. She thought she was still dreaming, so strange did it seem to her to feel herself being carried so high up in the air over the sea. By her side lay a cluster of pretty ripe berries and a bundle of sweet roots. Her youngest brother had gathered them for her and laid them there, and she thanked him with a smile, for she knew him as the Swan who flew over her head and shaded her with his wings.

They soared so high that the first ship they saw beneath them seemed like a white sea-gull hovering over the water. Elise saw behind her a large cloud, which looked like a mountain, and on it were gigantic shadows of herself and the eleven Swans; altogether it formed a picture more beautiful than any she had ever yet seen. Soon, however, the sun rose higher, the cloud was left behind, and the shadowy picture disappeared.

The whole day they flew on like a winged arrow through the air, but yet they went slower than usual, for they had their sister to carry. There seemed a storm brewing, and the evening was drawing near. Anxiously did Elise watch the sun. It was setting, and still the solitary rock could not be seen. It appeared to her that the Swans plied their wings faster and faster. Alas! it would be her fault if her brothers did not arrive at the rock in time. They would become human beings when the sun set, and must fall into the sea and be drowned. She prayed to God most fervently. Still no rock was to be seen. The black clouds drew nearer, and gusts of wind told of a coming storm, while from a mass of clouds that seemed to move forward like a leaden threatening wave flash after flash of lightning broke forth.

The sun was now on the rim of the sea. Elise's heart beat fast; the Swans shot downward so swiftly that she thought she must fall in, but another moment they began to soar again. The sun was half sunk beneath the water, but now she saw the little rock below her; it looked like a seal's head when he raises it just above the water. The sun was sinking fast. It seemed scarce larger than a star as her foot touched the hard ground, and in a moment it vanished altogether, like the last spark on a burnt piece of paper. Arm in arm her brothers stood around her; there was just room for her and them. The sea beat wildly against the rock, flinging over them a shower of foam. The sky seemed ablaze with the continual flashes, and one clap of thunder followed close on another, but sister and brothers kept firm hold of each other's hands. They sang a psalm, and their psalm gave them comfort and courage.

By daybreak the air was pure and still; and, as soon as the sun rose, the Swans flew away with Elise from the rock. The sea was still rough, and from the clouds the white foam that crested the blackish-green waves looked as if millions of swans were swimming on the waters.

As day advanced, Elise saw before her floating in the air a range of mountains, with masses of glittering ice on their summits. In their midst stood a castle at least a mile in length, with rows of columns, one above another, while around it grew palm-trees and gorgeous-looking flowers as large as mill-wheels. She asked if this was the land to which they were flying, but the Swans shook their heads, for what she saw was the beautiful ever-changing cloud castle of the fairy Morgana, which no human being can ever enter. Whilst Elise still bent her eyes upon it, mountains, trees, and castle all disappeared, and in their place stood twenty stately churches with high towers and pointed windows—she fancied she heard the organ play, but it was only the murmur of the sea. As they drew nearer to these churches they too changed into a large fleet sailing under them. She looked down and saw it was only a sea-mist passing rapidly over the water. Such strange scenes kept floating before her eyes, till at last she saw the actual land to which they were going with its blue mountains, its cedar woods, its towns, and castles. Long before sunset Elise sat down among the mountains, in front of a large cavern where delicate young creepers grew so thickly around that the ground appeared covered with gay embroidered carpets.

"Now we shall see what thou wilt dream of tonight!" said her youngest brother, as he showed her the chamber where she was to sleep.

"Oh that I could dream how you might be freed from the spell!" said she; and she could think of nothing else. She prayed most earnestly for God's help, nay, even in her dreams she continued praying, and it appeared to her that she was flying up high in the air towards the castle of the fairy Morgana. The fairy came forward to meet her, radiant and beautiful, and yet she thought she looked like the old woman who had given her berries in the forest, and told her of the Swans with golden crowns.

"You can release your brothers," said she; "but have you courage and patience enough? The water is indeed softer than your delicate hands, and yet can mould the hard stones to its will, but then it cannot feel the pain which your tender fingers will feel; it has no heart, and cannot suffer the anxiety and grief which you must suffer. Do you see these stinging-nettles I have in my hand? There are many round the cave where you are sleeping; only those that grow there or on the graves in the churchyard are of use, remember that! You must pluck them though they sting your hand; you must trample on them with your feet, and get yarn from them, and with this yarn you must weave eleven shirts with long sleeves. When they are all made, throw them over the eleven Wild Swans, and the spell will be broken. But mark: from the moment that you begin your work till it is completed, even should it occupy you for years, you must not speak a word. The first syllable that escapes your lips will fall like a dagger into the hearts of your brothers. On your tongue depends their life. Mark well all this!"

At the same moment the fairy touched Elise's hands with a nettle, which made them burn like fire, and Elise awoke. It was broad daylight, and close to her lay a nettle like the one she had seen in her dream. She fell upon her knees, thanked God, and then went out of the cave to begin her work. She plucked with her own delicate hands the ugly stinging-nettles. They burned large blisters on her hands and arms, but she bore the pain willingly in the hope of freeing her dear brothers. Then she trampled on the nettles with her naked feet, and spun the green yarn.

At sunset came her brothers. Elise's silence quite frightened them; they thought it must be the effect of some fresh spell of their wicked step-mother; but when they saw her blistered hands, they found out what their sister was doing for their sake. The youngest brother wept, and when his tears fell upon her hands, Elise felt no more pain, and the blisters disappeared.

The whole night she spent in her work, for she could not rest till she had released her brothers. All the following day she sat in her solitude, for the Swans had flown away; but never had time passed so quickly. One shirt was ready; and she now began the second.

Suddenly a hunting-horn echoed among the mountains and made her start with fear. The noise came nearer, she heard the hounds barking. In great terror she fled into the cave, bound up into a bundle the nettles she had gathered and combed, and sat down upon it.

She had just done so when a large dog sprang out from the bushes. Two others immediately followed; they barked loudly, ran away, and then returned. It was not long before the hunters stood in front of the cave. The handsomest among them was the King of that country; and he stepped up to Elise, for never had he seen a lovelier maiden.

"How came you here, beautiful child?" said he. Elise shook her head; she dared not speak, a word might have cost her the life of her brothers; and she hid her hands under her apron lest the King should see how she was suffering.

"Come with me," said he. "You must not stay here! If you are as good as you are beautiful, I will dress you in velvet and silk, I will put a gold crown upon your head and you shall dwell in my palace!" So he lifted her upon his horse, while she wept and wrung her hands; but the King said, "I only desire your happiness! You shall thank me for this some day!" and away he rode over mountains and valleys, holding her on his horse in front, whilst the other hunters followed. When the sun set, the King's capital with its churches and domes lay before them, and the King led Elise into the palace, where, in a high marble hall, fountains were playing, and the walls and ceiling were covered with the most beautiful paintings. But

Elise cared not for all this splendour; she wept and mourned in silence, even whilst some female attendants dressed her in royal robes, wove costly pearls into her hair, and drew soft gloves over her blistered hands.

And now as she stood before them in her rich dress, her beauty was so dazzling, that the courtiers all bowed low before her, and the King chose her for his bride, although the Archbishop shook his head, and whispered that the "beautiful lady of the wood was only a witch, who had blinded their eyes and bewitched the King's heart."

But the King did not listen; he ordered that music should be played. The most costly dishes were served up, and the loveliest maidens danced round the bride. She was led through fragrant gardens into magnificent halls, but not a smile was seen to play upon her lips or beam from her eyes. She looked the very picture of grief. The King then opened a small room next her bedroom. The floor was covered with costly green tapestry, and looked exactly like the cave in which she had been found. On it lay the bundle of yarn which she had spun from the nettles, and by the wall hung the shirt she had made. One of the hunters had brought all this, thinking there must be something wonderful in it.

"Here you may dream of your former home," said the King. "Here is the work you were doing there. Amid all your present splendour it may sometimes give you pleasure to fancy yourself there again."

When Elise saw what was so dear to her heart, she smiled, and the blood came back to her cheeks. She thought her brothers might still be freed from the spell, and she kissed the King's hand. He pressed her to his heart, and ordered the bells of all the churches in the city to be rung, to announce their marriage. The beautiful dumb maiden of the wood was to become the Queen of the land.

The Archbishop whispered evil words in the King's ear, but he paid no heed to them. He and Elise were married, and the Archbishop himself was obliged to put the crown upon her head. In his rage he pressed the narrow rim so firmly on her forehead that it hurt her; but a heavier weight of sorrow for her brothers lay upon her heart, and she did not feel bodily pain. She was still silent, because a single word would have killed her brothers; but her eyes beamed with heartfelt love to the King, so good and handsome, who had done so much to make her happy. She loved him more and more every day. Oh! how she wished she might tell him her sorrows; but she must remain silent, she could not speak until her work was finished! So she stole away every night, and went into the little room that was fitted up like the cave. There she worked at her shirts; but by the time she had begun the seventh, all her yarn was spent.

She knew that the nettles she needed grew in the churchyard, but she must gather them herself; and how to get them she knew not.

"Oh, what is the pain in my fingers compared with the anguish my heart suffers!" thought she. "I must venture to the churchyard; the good God will still watch over me!"

Fearful as though she were about to do something wrong, one moonlight night she crept down to the garden, and through the long avenues into the lonely road leading to the churchyard. She saw sitting on one of the broadest tombstones a number of ugly old witches. They took off their ragged clothes as if they were going to bathe, and digging with their long lean fingers into the fresh grass, drew up the dead bodies and devoured the flesh. Elise was obliged to pass close by them, and the witches fixed their wicked eyes upon her; but she repeated her prayer, gathered the stinging-nettles, and took them back with her into the palace. One person only had seen her. It was the Archbishop; he was awake when others slept. Now he felt sure that all was not right about the Queen: she must be a witch, who had, by her magic, won the hearts of the King and all the people.

In the Confessional he told the King what he had seen, and what he feared; and when the slanderous words came from his lips, the sculptured images of the saints shook their heads as though they would say, "It is untrue, Elise is innocent!" But the Archbishop explained the omen quite otherwise; he thought it was a testimony against her, and that the holy images shook their heads at hearing of her sin.

Two large tears rolled down the King's cheeks; and he returned home in doubt. He pretended to sleep at night, though sleep never visited him; and he noticed that Elise rose from her bed every night, and every time he followed her secretly and saw her enter her little room.

His face grew darker every day. Elise perceived it,

though she did not know the cause. She was much pained; and besides, what did she not suffer in her heart for her brothers! Her bitter tears ran down on the royal velvet and purple, looking like bright diamonds; and all who saw the grandeur that surrounded her wished themselves in her place. She had now nearly finished her work, only one shirt was wanting. Unfortunately, yarn was wanting also; she had not a single nettle left. Once more, only this one time, she must go to the the churchyard and gather a few handfuls. She shuddered when she thought of the solitary walk and of the horrid witches, but her resolution was as firm as her trust in God.

Elise went, and the King and the Archbishop followed her. They saw her disappear at the churchyard door; and when they came nearer they saw the witches sitting on the tombstones as Elise had seen them; and the King turned away, for he believed her whose head had rested on his bosom that very evening to be amongst them. "Let the people judge her!" said he. And the people condemned her to be burnt.

She was now dragged from the King's splendid palace into a dark, damp prison, where the wind whistled through the grated window. Instead of velvet and silk, they gave her the bundle of nettles she had gathered. On that she had to lay her head, and the shirts she had woven had to serve her as mattress and counterpane. But they could not have given her anything more welcome to her; and she continued her work, at the same time praying earnestly to God. The boys sang shameful songs about her in front of her prison; not a soul comforted her with one word of love.

Towards evening she heard the rustling of Swans' wings at the grating. It was the youngest of her brothers, who had at last found her, and she sobbed aloud for joy, although she knew that probably she had only one night to live; but then her work was almost finished and her brothers were near.

The Archbishop came in to spend the last hour with her as he had promised the King he would; but she shook her head and begged him with looks and signs to go away; for this night she must finish her work, or all she had suffered, her pain, her anxiety, her sleepless nights, would be in vain. The Archbishop went away with many angry words; but poor Elise knew herself to be perfectly innocent, and went on with her work.

Little mice ran busily about and dragged the nettles to her feet, wishing to help her; and a thrush perched on the iron bars of the window, and sang all night as merrily as he could, that she might not lose courage.

An hour before sunrise the eleven brothers stood before the palace gates, and begged to be shown to the King. But it could not be, they were told; it was still night, the King was asleep, and they dared not wake him. They prayed, they threatened in vain. The guard came up; at last the King himself stepped out to ask what was the matter; but at that moment the sun rose, the brothers could be seen no longer, and eleven white Swans flew away over the palace.

The people poured forth from the gates of the city to see the witch burnt. One wretched horse drew the cart in which Elise sat. She wore a coarse frock of sackcloth, her beautiful long hair hung loosely over her shoulders, her cheeks were of a deathly paleness; but her lips moved gently, and her fingers wove the green yarn, for even on her way to her cruel death she did not give up her work. The ten shirts lay at her feet, she was now labouring to complete the eleventh. The crowd insulted her.

"Look at the witch, how she mutters! She has no psalm book in her hand,—no, there she sits with her hateful juggling! Tear it from her, tear it into a thousand pieces!" And they all crowded about her, and were on the point of snatching away the shirts, when eleven white Swans came flying towards the cart, settled all round her, and flapped their wings. The crowd gave way in terror.

"It is a sign from Heaven! She is certainly innocent!" whispered some; they dared not say so aloud.

The executioner now took hold of her hand to lift her out of the cart, but she hastily threw the eleven shirts over the Swans, and eleven handsome Princes appeared in their place. The youngest had, however, only one arm, and a wing instead of the other, for one sleeve in his shirt had not been quite finished.

"Now I may speak," said she; "I am innocent!"

And the people who had seen what had happened bowed before her as before a saint. She, however, sank lifeless in her brothers' arms; suspense, fear, and grief had quite exhausted her.

"Yes, she is innocent," said her eldest brother, and he told their wonderful story. Whilst he spoke a fragrance as from millions of roses spread itself around, for every piece of wood in the funeral pile had taken root and sent forth branches, and a hedge of blooming red roses surrounded Elise, and above all the others blossomed a flower of a dazzling white colour, bright as a star. The King plucked it and laid it on Elise's bosom, and then she awoke with peace and joy in her heart.

And all the church bells began to ring of their own accord, and birds flew to the spot in swarms, and there was a joyous procession back to the palace, such as no king has ever seen equalled.

The Nightingale

The palace of the Emperor of China was the most beautiful palace in the world. It was made entirely of fine porcelain, which was so brittle that whoever touched it had to be very careful.

The choicest flowers were to be seen in the garden; and to the prettiest of these, little silver bells were fastened, in order that their tinkling might prevent any one from passing by without noticing them. Yes! everything in the Emperor's garden was wonderfully well arranged; and the garden itself stretched so far that even the gardener did not know the end of it. Whoever walked farther than the end of the garden, however, came to a beautiful wood with very high trees, and beyond that to the sea. The tall trees went down quite to the sea, which was very deep and blue, so that large ships could sail close under their branches; and among the branches dwelt a nightingale, who sang so sweetly that even the poor fishermen, who had so much else to do when they came out at night-time to cast their nets, would stand still to listen to her song.

Travellers came from all parts of the world to the Emperor's city, and they admired the city, the palace and the garden; but if they heard the nightingale they all said, "This is the best." And they talked about her after they went home, and learned men who wrote books about the city, the palace, and the garden, praised the nightingale above everything else. Poets also wrote the most beautiful verses about the nightingale of the wood near the sea.

These books went round the world, and one of them at last reached the Emperor. He read and read, and nodded his head every moment; for these splendid descriptions of the city, the palace, and the garden, pleased him greatly.

But at last he saw something that surprised him. The words "But the nightingale is the best of all" were written in the book.

"What in the world is this?" said the Emperor. "The nightingale! I do not know it at all! Can there be such a bird in my empire, in my garden even, without my having even heard of it? Truly one may learn something from books."

So he called his Prime Minister. Now this was so grand a personage that no one of inferior rank might speak to him; and if one did venture to ask him a question, his only answer was "Pooh!" which has no particular meaning.

"There is said to be a very remarkable bird here, called the nightingale," began the Emperor; "her song, they say, is worth more than anything else in all my dominions. Why has no one ever told me of her?"

"I have never before heard her mentioned," said the Prime Minister; "she has never been presented at court."

"I wish her to come and sing before me this evening," said the Emperor. "The whole world, it seems, knows what I have, better than I do myself!"

"I have never before heard her mentioned," said the Prime Minister, "but I will seek her, and try to find her."

But where was she to be found? The Prime Minister

ran up one flight of steps, down another, through halls, and through passages, but not one of all the people he met had ever heard of the nightingale. So he went back to the Emperor, and said, "It must be a fable invented by the man who wrote the book. Your Imperial Majesty must not believe all that is written in books; much in them is pure invention."

"But the book in which I have read it," said the Emperor, "was sent me by the high and mighty Emperor of Japan, and therefore it cannot be untrue. I wish to hear the nightingale; she must be here this evening; and if she does not come, after supper the whole court shall be flogged."

In great alarm, the Prime Minister again ran up stairs and down stairs, through halls and through passages; and half the court ran with him; for no one liked the idea of being flogged. Many were the questions asked about the wonderful nightingale, of whom the whole world talked, and about whom no one at court knew anything.

At last they met a poor little girl in the kitchen, who said, "Oh yes! the nightingale! I know her very well. Oh! how she can sing! Every evening I carry the fragments left at table to my poor sick mother. She lives by the seashore; and when I am coming back, and stay to rest a little in the wood, I hear the nightingale sing. It makes the tears come into my eyes!"

"Little kitchen-maiden," said the Prime Minister, "I will get you a good place in the kitchen, and you shall have permission to see the Emperor dine, if you will take us to the nightingale; for she is expected at court this evening."

So they went together to the wood where the nightingale was accustomed to sing, and half the court went with them. Whilst they were on the way, a cow began to low.

"Oh!" said the court pages, "now we have her! It is certainly a wonderfull voice for so small an animal; surely we have heard it somewhere before."

"No, those are cows you hear lowing," said the little kitchen-maid; "we are still far from the place."

The frogs were now croaking in the pond.

"There she is now!" said the chief court-preacher; "her voice sounds just like little church-bells."

"No, those are frogs," said the little kitchen-maid, "but we shall soon hear her."

Then the nightingale began to sing.

"There she is!" said the little girl; "listen! listen! There she sits," she added, pointing to a little grey bird up in the branches.

"Is it possible?" said the Prime Minister. "I should not have thought it. How simple she looks! She must certainly have changed colour at the sight of so many distinguished personages."

"Little nightingale!" called out the kitchen-maid, "our gracious Emperor wishes you to sing something to him."

"With the greatest pleasure," said the nightingale, and she sang so beautifully that every one was enchanted.

"It sounds like glass bells," said the Prime Minister. "And look at her little throat, how it moves! It is singular that we should never have heard her before; she will have great success at court."

"Shall I sing again to the Emperor?" asked the nightingale, for she thought the Emperor was among them.

"Most excellent nightingale!" said the Prime Minister, "I have the honour to invite you to a court festival, which is to take place this evening, when His Imperial Majesty will be delighted to hear you sing."

"My song would sound far better among the green trees," said the nightingale; but she followed willingly when she heard that the Emperor wished it.

In the centre of the grand hall where the Emperor sat, a golden perch had been fixed, on which the nightingale was to sit. The whole court was present, and the little kitchen-maid received permission to stand behind the door, for she now had the rank and title of "Maid of the Kitchen". All were dressed in their finest clothes; and all eyes were fixed upon the little grey bird, to whom the Emperor nodded as a signal for her to begin.

The nightingale sang so sweetly that tears came into the Emperor's eyes and tears rolled down his cheeks. Then the nightingale sang more sweetly still, and touched the hearts of all who heard her; and the Emperor was so pleased that he said, "The nightingale shall have my golden slippers, and wear them round her neck." But the nightingale thanked him, and said she was already sufficiently rewarded.

"I have seen tears in the Emperor's eyes; that is the greatest reward I can have. The tears of an Emperor have a special value. I feel myself highly honoured." And then she sang again more charmingly than ever.

"That singing is the most charming gift ever known,"

said the ladies present; and they put water into their mouths, and tried when they spoke to move their throats as she did. They thought to become nightingales also. Indeed, even the footmen and chamber-maids declared that they were quite satisfied; which was a great thing to say, for of all people they are the most difficult to please. Yes indeed! the nightingale's success was complete. She was now to remain at court, to have her own cage, with permission to fly out twice in the day and once in the night. Twelve servants were set apart to wait on her on these occasions, who were each to hold the end of a silken band fastened round her foot. There was not much pleasure in that kind of flying.

All the city was talking of the wonderful bird; and when two people met, one would say only "nightin" and the other "gale"; and then they sighed, and understood each other perfectly. Indeed, eleven of the children of the citizens were named after the nightingale; but not one of them could sing a note.

One day a large parcel arrived for the Emperor, on which was written "The Nightingale".

"Here we have another new book about our far-famed bird," said the Emperor. But it was not a book; it was a little piece of mechanism lying in a box—an artificial nightingale, which was intended to look like the living one, but covered all over with diamonds, rubies, and sapphires. When this artificial bird had been wound up, it could sing one of the tunes that the real nightingale sang; and its tail, all glittering with silver and gold, went up and down all the time.

"That is splendid!" said every one; and he who had brought the bird was given the title of "Chief Imperial Nightingale Bringer".

Then the Emperor ordered that the real and the toy nightingales should sing together. But it did not succeed, for the real nightingale sang in her own natural way, and the artificial bird produced its tones by wheels.

"It is not his fault," said the music master; "he keeps exact time, and quite according to method."

So the artificial bird now sang alone. He was quite as successful as the real nightingale; and then he was so much prettier to look at—his plumage sparkled like jewels.

Three and thirty times he sang one and the same tune, and yet he was not weary. Every one would willingly have heard him again. The Emperor, however, now wished the real nightingale to sing something—but where was she? No one had noticed that she had flown out of the open window—flown away to her own green wood.

"What is the meaning of this?" said the Emperor; and all the courtiers abused the nightingale, and called her a most ungrateful creature. "We have the best bird at all events," said they, and for the four and thirtieth time they heard the same tune, but still they did not quite know it, because it was so difficult. The music master praised the bird very highly; indeed, he declared it was superior to the real nightingale in every way.

"For see," he said, "with the real nightingale one could never reckon on what was coming, but everything is settled with the artificial bird. He will sing in this one way, and no other. This can be proved; he can be taken to pieces, and the works can be shown—where the wheels lie, how they move, and just how one follows from another."

"That is just what I think," said everybody; and the artist received permission to show the bird to the people on the following Sunday. "They too shall hear him sing," the Emperor said. So they heard him, and were as well pleased as if they had all been drinking tea; for it is tea that makes the Chinese merry. But the fisherman who had heard the real nightingale, said, "It sounds very pretty, almost like the real bird; but yet there is something wanting, I do not know what."

The real nightingale was banished from the empire.

The artificial bird had his place on a silken cushion, close to the Emperor's bed; all the presents he received, gold and precious stones, lay around him. He had been given the rank and title of "High Imperial Toilet Singer."

And the music master wrote five and twenty volumes about the artificial bird, with the longest and most difficult words that are to be found in the Chinese language. So, of course, all said they had read and understood them, otherwise they would have been stupid, and perhaps would have been flogged.

Thus it went on for a year. The Emperor, the court, and all the Chinese knew every note of the artificial bird's song by heart; but that was the very reason why they enjoyed it so much—they could now sing with him. The little boys in the street sang "zizizi, cluck, cluck, cluck!" and the Emperor himself sang too.

But one evening, when the bird was in full voice and the Emperor lay in bed and listened, suddenly there was a "whizz" inside the bird. Then a spring cracked. "Whir-r-r-r" went all the wheels running round; and the music stopped.

The Emperor jumped quickly out of bed, and had his chief physician called; but of what use could he be? Then a clockmaker was fetched; and at last, after a great deal of discussion and consultation, the bird was in some measure put to rights again; but the clockmaker said he must be spared much singing, for the pegs were almost worn out, and it was impossible to put in new ones, at least without spoiling the music.

There was great lamentation, for now the artificial bird was allowed to sing only once a year, and even then there were difficulties. However, the music master made a short speech full of his favourite long words, and said the bird was as good as ever; and, of course, no one contradicted him.

When five years were passed away, a great affliction visited the whole empire, for the Emperor was ill, and it was reported that he could not live. A new Emperor had already been chosen, and the people stood in the street, outside the palace, and asked the Prime Minister how the Emperor was.

"Pooh!" said he, and shook his head.

Cold and pale lay the Emperor in his magnificent bed. All the court believed him to be already dead, and every one ran away to greet the new Emperor.

But the Emperor was not yet dead. He could scarcely

breathe, however, and it appeared to him as though something was sitting on his chest. He opened his eyes, and saw that it was Death. He had put on the Emperor's crown, and in one hand held the golden scimitar and in the other the splendid imperial banner. From under the folds of the thick velvet hangings the strangest-looking heads were peering forth, some with very ugly faces, and others with looks that were extremely gentle and lovely. These were the bad and good deeds of the Emperor, which were now all fixing their eyes upon him, whilst Death sat on his heart.

"Do you know this?" they whispered one after another. "Do you remember that?" And they began reproaching him in such a manner that the sweat broke out upon his forehead.

"I have never known anything like it," said the Emperor. "Music, music, the great Chinese drum!" cried he; "let me not hear what they are saying."

They went on, however; and Death, quite in the Chinese fashion, nodded his head to every word.

"Music, music!" cried the Emperor. "You dear little golden bird! sing, I pray you, sing!—I have given you gold and precious stones. I have even hung my golden slippers round your neck—sing, I pray you, sing!"

But the bird was silent. There was no one there to wind him up; and without that he could not sing. Death continued to stare at the Emperor with his great hollow eyes! And everywhere it was still, fearfully still!

All at once came the sweetest music through the window. It was the little living nightingale who was sitting on a branch outside. She had heard of her Emperor's severe illness, and was come to sing to him of comfort and hope. As she sang, the spectral forms became paler and paler; the blood flowed more and more quickly through the Emperor's feeble members; and even Death listened, and aid, "Go on, little nightingale, go on."

"Will you give me the beautiful golden sword? Will you give me the rich banner? and will you give me the Emperor's crown?" said the bird.

And Death gave up all these treasures for a song. And the nightingale sang on. She sang of the quiet churchyard where white roses blossom, where the lilac sends forth its fragrance, and the fresh grass is bedewed with the tears of the sorrowing friends of the departed. Then Death was seized with a longing to see his garden, and, like a cold white shadow, flew out at the window.

"Thanks, thanks, little bird," said the Emperor, "I know you well. I banished you from my realm, and you have sung away those evil faces from my bed, and death from my heart. How can I reward you?"

"You have already rewarded me," said the nightingale; "I have seen tears in your eyes, as when I sang to you for the first time. Those I shall never forget; they are the jewels that gladden a minstrel's heart! But sleep now and wake fresh and healthy. I will sing to you again."

And she sang—and the Emperor fell into a sweet sleep. Oh, how soft and refreshing it was!

The sun shone in at the window when he awoke, strong and healthy. Not one of his servants had returned, for they all believed him dead; only the nightingale still sat beside him and sang.

"You shall always stay with me," said the Emperor. "You shall only sing when it pleases you, and the artificial bird I will break into a thousand pieces."

"Do not so," said the nightingale; "he has done what he could; take care of him. I cannot stay in the palace; but let me come when I like. I will sit on the branches close to the window, in the evening, and sing to you, that you may become happy and have thoughts full of joy. I will sing to you of those who rejoice and of those who suffer. I will sing to you of all that is good or bad which is hidden from you. The little minstrel flies afar to the fisherman's hut, to the peasant's cottage, to all who are far distant from you and your court. I love your heart more than your crown, and yet the crown has an odour of some-thing holy about it. I will come; I will sing. But you must promise me one thing."

"Everything," said the Emperor. And he stood in his imperial splendour, which he had put on himself, and held to his heart the scimitar so heavy with gold.

"One thing I beg of you: let no one know that you have a little bird who tells you everything; then all will go well." And the nightingale flew away.

The attendants came in to look at their dead Emperor— and the Emperor said "Good-morning!"

The Rose-Elf

Standing in the middle of a garden grew a rose-tree covered with lovely roses, and in one of these, the loveliest
of all, dwelt a little elf. He was so very little that no
human eye could see him. He had a sleeping-room behind each rose-leaf. He was fair and slender as only a
child can be, and had wings that reached from his shoulders to his feet. Oh! what a sweet odour there was in his
chambers, and how clean and beautiful the walls were!
They were the pale pink rose-leaves.

He spent the whole day basking in the warm sunshine,
flying from flower to flower, dancing on the wings of
flying butterflies, and reckoning how many steps it took
him to run over all the roads and footpaths of a single
lime-leaf; for what we call the veins of the leaf were to
him roads and footpaths, and he found them almost endless. The sun set before he had ended his journey. He had
set off too late.

It grew very cold; the dew fell fast, the wind blew, the
best thing he could do was to hurry home. But though he
made all the haste he could the roses were all closed; and
he could not get in—not a single rose was open. The
poor little elf was greatly frightened. He had never before been out in the night air, but had always slept sweetly
and softly behind the warm rose-leaves. Certainly, this
night would be the death of him!

At the other end of the garden he knew that there was

an arbour of honeysuckles, whose flowers looked like great painted horns. So he made up his mind to get into one of these, and sleep there till morning. Accordingly, he flew to the spot. But hush!—there were two persons in the arbour—a handsome young man and a beautiful girl. They sat close together, wishing that they might never need to part again: they loved each other so much, more than the best child can love his father and mother.

"And yet we must part!" said the young man. "Your brother hates us, and that is why he sends me far away on business over the mountains, and across the ocean. Farewell, my sweet bride, for surely you are my bride!"

Then they kissed each other, and the young girl wept, and gave him a rose: but before giving it to him she pressed on it a kiss so warm that the flower opened, and the little elf flew in and leant his head against the delicate, fragrant walls. He could hear distinctly the words, "Farewell, farewell!" and he felt that the rose was placed in the young man's bosom. Oh, how the heart was throbbing! The little elf could not sleep at all for hearing the beats. The rose was not suffered to remain long in its warm resting-place. The man soon took it out, and whilst walking alone through the dark wood he kissed the flower so often and so vehemently that our tiny elf was well-nigh squeezed to death. He could feel through the rose-leaves how the man's lips were burning, and the rose opened more and more, just as though the hot midday sun were shining upon it.

But there came another man through the wood, looking gloomy and wrathful. It was the beautiful girl's wicked brother. He drew out a sharp knife, and, while the lover was kissing the rose, stabbed him to the heart, cut off his head, and buried both head and body in the moist earth under a lime-tree.

"Now we are rid of him!" thought the wicked brother; "and he will never come back again. He was to have taken a long journey over the mountains and beyond the sea; men often lose their lives in travelling as he has done! He will never come back again, and my sister dare not question me about him."

So he scraped with his foot some withered leaves over the upturned earth, and then walked home through the darkness. But he did not go alone, as he thought; the tiny elf went with him, rolled up in a withered lime-leaf which had fallen into the wicked man's hair while he was digging the grave. The man put on his hat, and then it was dark for our little elf, who was underneath, trembling with horror and indignation at the shameful deed he had witnessed.

In the early morning the wicked man reached his home. He took off his hat, and went into his sister's sleeping-room. The bright and beautiful girl lay there dreaming of him whom she loved so well, and who, she supposed, was now wandering far away across mountain and forest. Her wicked brother bent over her, and laughed a hateful laugh, a laugh like that of a fiend. The withered leaf fell out of his hair upon the counterpane, but he did not notice it, and went away intending to sleep a little himself in the early morning hours. The elf now glided out of the withered leaf, crept to the ear of the sleeping girl, and told her, as though in a dream, all about the horrible murder. He described to her the spot where her brother had slain her lover, and had buried the body, close under the lime-trees in full blossom, and added: "In token that all I have told you is not a mere dream, you shall find a withered leaf upon your bed when you awake."

Oh, what bitter tears she shed when she awoke and found the withered lime-leaf on her bed! But she dared not speak to any one of her great sorrow. The window was left open all day, so that the little elf could easily have flown out to the roses and other flowers in the garden; but he could not find it in his heart to leave one who was so unhappy. A monthly rose-tree stood at the window; he got into one of its flowers, and sat looking at the poor girl. Her brother often came into the room, and seemed very merry, but she dared not speak a word to him of her heart's sorrow.

As soon as it was night she stole out of the house, and going to the wood, to the place where the lime-tree grew, she swept away the dry leaves, and dug in the earth till she found the corpse of the murdered man. Oh, how she wept and prayed to God that she too might die soon!

Gladly would she have taken the body home with her, but that she could not do. So she took up the head, kissed the pale, cold lips and closed eyes, and shook the earth out of the beautiful hair. "This I will keep!" said she, and covering the dead body afresh with earth, she returned home, taking with her the head and a little bough from a jasmine-tree that blossomed near the grave. When she reached home she fetched the largest flower-pot she could find, put into it the head of the dead man, covered it over with mould, and planted the slip of jasmine above it.

"Farewell, farewell!" whispered the little elf. He could no longer bear to witness so much misery, and he flew into the garden to his own rose. But he found it faded, and only a few pale leaves still clinging to the green hedge behind. "Alas! how quickly does everything good and beautiful pass away!" sighed the elf. At last he found another rose that would suit for his home, and laid himself down among its fragrant leaves. And he flew every morning to the window of the poor girl's room, and every morning he found her standing over the flower-pot weeping. Her salt tears fell upon the jasmine, and day by day, as she grew paler and paler, the plant grew fresher and greener. One little shoot after another pushed forth, and the delicate white buds unfolded into flowers. And she kissed the flowers; but her wicked brother mocked her, and asked her if she had lost her wits. He could not bear it, and he could not understand why she was always weeping over that Jasmine. He did not know whose closed eyes were resting there, nor whose red lips were fading beneath the earth

One day she leaned her head against the flower-pot, and the little rose-elf flew into the room and found her sleeping. He crept into her ear, and talked to her of what he had heard in the arbour on that sad evening, of the fragrance of the roses, and of the love that the flower-spirits bore her. She dreamed very sweetly, and while she was dreaming her life slipped away calmly and gently, and her spirit, now at perfect peace, was in heaven with him whom she had loved so dearly.

And the blossoms of the jasmine opened their large white bells, and sent forth a fragrance wonderfully sweet and strong; this was the only way in which they could bewail the dead.

But the wicked brother saw the beautiful, blooming tree, and considering it now his own, he took it away into his sleeping-room and placed it near the bed, for it was very beautiful and its fragrance was delightful. The little rose-elf followed it, flew from flower to flower, for in each flower there dwelt a little spirit, and to each he told of the murdered young man whose head was now dust with the dust under their roots, of the wicked brother and the heartbroken sister.

"We know it!" replied all the spirits of the flowers; "we know it! Have not we sprung from the eyes and lips of the murdered man? We know it, we know it!" And they all nodded their heads in the strangest manner.

The rose-elf could not understand how they could take it so quietly, and he flew away to the bees, who were gathering honey in the garden, and told the story to them. And the bees told their Queen, and she gave orders that next morning they should all go and kill the murderer.

That very same night, however—it was the first night after his sister's death—whilst the brother was asleep in the bed near which the jasmine-tree was placed, each little flower-cup opened, and out flew the flower-spirits, invisible, but armed each with a poisoned arrow. They first crept into his ear and made him dream of his sinful deed, and then flew through his parted lips, and stabbed him in the tongue with their poisonous shafts.

"Now we have avenged the dead!" said they, and they flew back into the white jasmine-cups.

After day had dawned, the bedroom window being suddenly flung open, the rose-elf flew in, followed by the Queen-bee and her whole swarm; they had come to sting the murderer to death. But he was already dead; some persons were standing round the bed, declaring, "The strong scent of the jasmines has killed him!"

The rose-elf then understood that the flower-spirits had taken vengeance on the murderer. He explained it to the Queen-bee, and she, with her whole swarm, buzzed round the flower-pot in token of approval. In vain did people try to drive them off. At last a man took up the flower-pot, intending to carry it away, whereupon one of the bees stung him in the hand, so that the pot fell to the ground and broke in pieces.

All who were present then saw the beautiful curling hair of the murdered youth, and guessed that the dead man in the bed must be a murderer.

And the Queen-bee flew buzzing about in the garden, singing of the vengeance of the flowers, of the rose-elf, and how that behind the tiniest leaf there lurks a spirit who knows when crime is committed, and can punish the evil-doer.